Vlad
the Undead

Vlad
the Undead

Hanna Lützen

A Groundwood Book
Douglas & McIntyre
Toronto Vancouver Buffalo

Groundwood Books/Douglas & McIntyre
585 Bloor Street West, Toronto, Ontario M6G 1K5

Distributed in the U.S.A. by Publishers Group West
1700 Fourth Street, Berkeley, CA 94710

We acknowledge the financial support of the Canada Council for the
Arts, the Ontario Arts Council and the Government of Canada
through the Book Publishing Industry Development Program for our
publishing activities.

Library of Congress data is available

Canadian Cataloguing in Publication Data
Lützen, Hanna, 1962-
Vlad the undead
Translation of: Vlad
ISBN 0-88899-341-2 (bound) ISBN 0-88899-342-0 (pbk.)
1. Dracula, Count (Fictitious character) —
Juvenile fiction. I. Title.
PZ7.L988Vl 1998   j833'.92   C98-931111-2

Design by Michael Solomon
Cover illustration by Harvey Chan
Printed and bound in Canada by Webcom Ltd.

PREFACE

Returning home after several months abroad, I discovered these documents. I had expected that my niece, Lucia, who had been staying in my apartment since the sudden and tragic deaths of her parents, would be here to greet me at my homecoming, but she had disappeared without a trace — except for the strange tale written on these oddly yellowed papers. I now present her narrative as I found it, for I desperately wish to share her thoughts and actions prior to her disappearance in the summer of 1994 with anyone sympathetic to my tragic and inexplicable loss. Perhaps, by letting other readers enter her dark and bewildering world, I shall find comfort in the thought that Lucia's urge to express herself beyond the limits of reason has been acknowledged by others.

The story's headlines are written by me in an attempt to give some sort of order to the medley of voices that make up this book.

May 5, 1995
Wilhelm Mørck

Whitby, England
March 25, 1994

My dear granddaughter,

I have, as you well know, been ill for some time now. I am an old man and I know that it will not be long before I must depart this world. Therefore I leave you my old briefcase — the one I wouldn't let you touch when you were here last Christmas. You asked me why I always guarded those old papers so fiercely. Well, I had my reasons, as I also have a reason to present them all to you now. The briefcase will be waiting for you in the old bureau.

What now belongs to you is an old mariner's tale, told on the verge of death. His name was Josef Maresciu, captain of the schooner *Demeter*, which was stranded outside Whitby harbor in 1894. I was told that he was the only survivor aboard the ship except for an immense wolflike dog that leapt on shore when the wreck was towed in. They found the captain tied to the wheel in a deathlike swoon. He was soaking wet and cold as ice. His hair and face were grimed with salt, and the rope around his wrists had cut deeply into the poor man's flesh. It was nothing short of a miracle that he was still breathing.

They took him to the nearest doctor — my father and your great-grandfather, Lars Holmestad.

Here he was cared for until he died of exhaustion. Before he died he told the grisly tale of the last voyage of the *Demeter*. Your great-grandfather wrote down every word at his patient's request.

Whether the story is the delirious ravings of a dying man or the true report of the events leading to the sad ending of the ship and its crew, I cannot say. I only know that the captain's log, which was given to the authorities upon the arrival of the *Demeter*, appeared enigmatic and incomplete. Perhaps Maresciu's last words form the complete explanation. Perhaps not. Anyway, the tale was never presented to the public or to the authorities of Whitby.

Only your great-grandfather and I have read these old papers. My father didn't tell anyone what he had learned. He only told me about Maresciu and his tale shortly before his death. Of course I already knew about the shipwreck in 1894. The event was one of Whitby's innumerable old wives' tales, but when my father passed the mariner's story on to me, I felt it to be the truth about the last voyage of the *Demeter*. It was both fascinating and frightening.

My father hadn't been able to decide what to do with the papers. As a faithful Christian he had to dismiss the tale as pure insanity, but some small part of him must have clung to the captain's words. He decided to keep it a secret but he never reached any understanding of the nature of Maresciu's confession. He chose to let me decide what to make of it and, not having reached any further enlightenment in the case, I now pass it on to you.

I have spent many years pondering over the papers. I could have destroyed them, or I could have turned them over to the folklorists in Whitby. I did neither because something in the story held me in a respectful and fearsome state of mind. I will not dismiss what I do not understand, but I can step away from the mystery and leave it to a fresher mind to work out. Perhaps you will be able to make sense of it, Lucia.

Do with it what you want. Take care and don't forget

your grandfather,
John Holmestad.

LETTER, LUCIA HOLMESTAD TO JOHN HOLMESTAD

Copenhagen, Denmark
April 4, 1994

Dearest Grandfather,
You know that I love to get a letter from you, but I must admit that your tone of voice made me sad.

What is the concept of time and age? Nothing but a prison for our minds? Nothing is ending. On the contrary, you have helped me make a new start since the accident. We have lived through the first year and I still need you. Mother and Father are gone. Please, don't you leave me, too.

Do you remember the story you used to tell me when I was a child? You told me about the girl who went to the troll's magic mountain because she wanted to find eternity. Her mother had told her that mountains stand for ever and ever. The troll welcomed her and said that he would indeed show her eternity. The girl stayed with him in his castle of rocks and she danced for him every night. She completely forgot about time. In fact, time didn't exist in the troll's castle. But one day she understood that she had made a terrible mistake. Eternity had stolen everything from her. She could never return to her home because her family and home had been erased by time. She was still as young as ever, but out in the world, time had changed every bit of what she used to love. She had settled herself in eternity, but eternity is different from time. Eternity is a pond of great stillness and depth. Time is a hurricane traveling with immense speed. She knew that she had to stay in the mountains and remain the same for ever. She was alone but she had become unchangeable and incorruptible. She understood eternity.

I can't help thinking of this story, and I wish

that you and I could just go up into the mountains and stay there for ever. You could tell me stories the way you used to, over and over again. And we would always stay the same, just like the girl and the troll.

It disturbs me that you've decided to show me your "secret documents." For a long time I've practically ached to see them. You really know how to keep me in suspense, but I don't understand what can be so strange that it must be hidden. You always used to tell me stories, so why keep this one from me? I'll bet it's a good one! And you may be right. Perhaps my view will be completely different from yours and great-grandfather's. I can hardly wait to see this "dark secret" of yours, and it won't be long before I arrive in good old Whitby again. School will be over by the end of May and I'll leave shortly after.

Now that I've settled down here in Uncle Wille's apartment I feel absolutely fine. He has only been home on short visits a couple of times but I do love his company, even if he's clearly thinking of some exotic bug or some strange, uninhabited island. But I don't mind being here alone. I like living in the heart of Copenhagen and inside this old building it feels like time has been suspended. Wille's place has decades of dust lying everywhere, and all the furniture is in the most charming Victorian style, which fits the fine stucco and the high moldings in here perfectly. It is almost a maze because the entire building is made with a stunning absence of method. Doors and corridors, rooms in succession and hidden chambers, not to mention the many walk-in closets big enough to hide several elephants. You can almost forget the day and age outside, because even the view from the windows is medieval. I can see Christian IV's Round Tower, the University of Copenhagen and the old students' residence. I feel at home, which indeed I am. Wille has invited me to live here for as long as I like, since he spends almost all his time abroad.

I've already gotten acquainted with his library of moldy old books and his collection of well-preserved dead insects. Have I told you that I am taking care of Delifrena for him? I don't mind having her as company. In fact, I'm very pleased that he has given me the honor of being nanny to his favorite live specimen.

Dear Grandfather, take care and be well until I arrive.

Lucia

LUCIA HOLMESTAD'S DIARY

May 15, 1994

Grandfather died last night.

Wille won't make it to the funeral. He's busy examining a freak specimen of *Psalmopæus cambridgei*. What can I say? Martinique is a wonderful place and I'm sure that a funeral in Whitby seems very unimportant and distant when you are in the midst of interesting work. Wille, you are a shit! I must go alone. I'll be there tonight.

Grandfather was buried yesterday.

I have to stay one more day. I have some things to attend to. Gretha has been wonderful the last few days, and I know Grandfather thought very highly of her. She took care of everything for him and kept his big old house in perfect order. She gave me the old briefcase right after I arrived. Apparently Grandfather had been very anxious that no one but me should see it, and poor Gretha just couldn't relax until it was safely tucked away in my suitcase. I wonder what the old sailor had to tell. I'm leaving tomorrow night.

Dear Grandfather,
The semester is over and I have a couple of

months to prepare for my final year in medical school. Now I want to spend time reading Maresciu's tale. I started looking at the old papers on the plane, but it occurred to me that this old story deserves my full attention, so I decided to wait. I wanted to read it carefully in the silence of Wille's library.

Now I'm back. Safe and sound and ready to plunge into the raving sailor's story. You wrote that a younger reader may be able to read it and reach a completely different understanding of the words. I don't know about that yet, but I will be sure to write down my impressions. My diary is solely dedicated to you, dear Grandfather.

JOSEF MARESCIU'S TALE

August 8, 1894

I, Lars Holmestad, write on behalf of my patient Josef Maresciu. I have no part in what these pages will reveal. I am merely providing the pen for a dying man so that he can communicate his last words.

◆

My name is Josef Maresciu. I am, or was, captain of the schooner *Demeter*. She and I have been traveling companions for a long time and now our last journey — from Varna to Whitby — is over. We will both be buried here. We have been faithful to each other until this sad ending. For it was not the sea that broke us down but even stronger powers. An unnatural and immense force destroyed my crew and my ship, and just the thought of the real nature of this pestilence makes me shudder. I could not bring myself to write this in the log. It seemed too unreal at the time. But it is my hope that I will find peace in my grave by revealing everything now. May God be my witness that this is my confession and the true story of the *Demeter's* last voyage.

We were ready for departure from Varna on July 6, 1894. The cargo was safely on board — mineral samples and forty-nine big boxes of dark soil as well as some kind of scientific testing material. I had a crew of five sailors, a cook and a mate. All eager to set sails and take off while the fresh east wind blew.

That was how I started my report in the log. Not completely untrue but not the whole truth, either. You see, two days before we left Varna, a man came to see me. He wanted to go to England. I told him that the *Demeter* was not built for a leisure cruise and suggested he look for one of the numerous passenger ships. For my part, I did not care much for the unavoidable problems a passenger would cause.

But he insisted. He told me that he was a scientist and that he was personally responsible for the forty-nine boxes of Roumanian soil. He wanted to keep an eye on this precious cargo until it was safely delivered. He assured me that he would pay handsomely.

Even at this hour I am not sure what made me give in to this strange character. The sum of money he offered was indeed very large, and it would, by my humble standards, make me a wealthy man for as long as I lived. But it was not entirely the money that made me consent. When I faced him, I felt oddly weak and confused. Maybe it was his eyes — almost glaring but strangely devoid of any emotion.

I said yes.

Now he presented his conditions. He wanted complete secrecy and the comfort that only the captain's quarters could offer. He emphasized that it should simply be announced that he was traveling as my guest. The crew need not know anything more about him and his purposes. The question of money was to be a private matter.

These conditions, put forward with stern authority, made me wince. He was ordering me about as his underling. But the money (as I then chose to believe, only the money) — 1500 pounds — made me bite my tongue. Or was it the man himself who exercised power over my will? I did feel pushed into the agreement, but I could not put my finger on anything but my own susceptibility to bribery. Nor was I able to justify my vague uneasiness about the man. He was about sixty years old, well dressed and very eloquent. There was an unmistakable aura of nobility about him, and his aquiline nose, white hair and well-trimmed moustache gave him the look of a distinguished scholar. In short, he looked highly respectable.

We hastily drew up an agreement. My guest now seemed very anxious to have my full consent and understanding of every paragraph in the document. His eager pleasantness took me by surprise, as his former conduct had been one of haughty, almost bidding sternness. I did not give this behavior a second thought, though I could not help wondering why he only signed our agreement with the initials V.D. He did not offer any explanation but remarked that there would be plenty of time to get properly acquainted.

We finished our business by settling the practical details. He asked me to prepare my inner cabin for his convenience and told me that he would be spending most of the time in there. He would only come out when nature called, as he put it. Then he made a quick bow and departed.

As planned, we set sail on July 6th. The weather was fine and the crew cheerful.

We entered the Bosporus, continued through the Dardanelles and soon reached the Aegean Sea. My guest kept to himself for the first couple of days. He did not come on deck, but I had the pleasure of his company when I had dinner served in my quarters. I invited him to join me but he declined. He explained that he had to keep a very strict diet consisting of special ingredients that he provided for himself. But he sat down for a while before retiring. He told me that he valued the privacy of the inner cabin as he had a lot of preparations to deal with before reaching England.

He was pleasant company. His conversation was interesting and revealed great knowledge of navigation and seamanship. I began to think very highly of this man. His mysterious secretiveness did not matter to me anymore. He had the right to choose when to tell me about himself.

The first week went by without problems of any kind. But, as I also noted in the log, the crew was growing steadily more anxious. They seemed scared, but neither I, nor the mate, could find out what was causing this. The only answer the mate could come up with was "There is something alien and hostile on board."

I knew that the crew disliked my guest and the anxiety was probably caused by some resentment toward his presence on the *Demeter*. They found him mysterious and suspicious, and everybody was guessing at the reason for his journey. I had, as agreed, only told them that he was my guest. Nothing else.

However, I could not report his presence in the log. I had received a very large sum of money from him, which could bring me in grave conflict with the Swedish shipping company that owned the *Demeter*. Therefore my explanation in the log remained meaningless: "unexplained excitement among the crew." This petty trouble seemed both unnecessary and irritating, so I gave the mate full authority to punish any troublemaker harshly. A couple of days later he lost his temper. The crew was behaving in a strange, agitated and deeply unconcentrated manner and the mate punished two men. I expected some kind of rebellious reaction, but nothing happened. The men went back to their chores and gave the work their full attention. I noticed that they crossed themselves every now and then, without any obvious reason.

My guest kept to himself as usual and did not seem alarmed by the disturbance among the crew that he, involuntarily, had caused. One night as we sat together at my dinner table, he told me that he was getting quite seasick and would probably have to keep to his cabin for the next couple of days. It must have been around July 16. He said that he was not used to the constant rolling and turning of the ship but otherwise his spirits seemed high. This was a very natural reaction and I promised him that he would be left alone.

The next morning I was awakened by a great noise and hubbub on deck. Sailor Abramoff was missing. Vanished from the ship.

Abramoff had served the middle watch and had been the sole man on deck for hours. At dawn the relief watch had found nothing but an empty deck. We searched the ship several times but did not find any trace of the man. No one could explain his disappearance.

I ignored the men's mutterings about the jinx in my quarters and simply made a note of the sad and shocking disappearance of Abramoff in the log: "Man overboard. Nervous breakdown followed by accident." What else could have happened? Nobody had seen or heard anything unusual during the night.

It is dangerous to let unfounded suspicions get the better of you at sea, so I made it very clear that we could not accuse anyone of having part in this unfortunate matter. Abramoff was one of the men who had been punished by the mate. I took full responsibility for not having observed his mental state at the time.

It turned out that I completely misjudged the situation on board, and my lack of apprehension cost us dearly.

The following day one of the men, Olgaren, came to see me. He was in a terrible state and rambled on about some ghastly vision he had experienced during his night watch. He was absolutely certain that we had some kind of unearthly stowaway on the ship. Around midnight he had seen a tall man step out on deck. It was raining heavily with cold gusts of wind sweeping the waves, and Olgaren had sought shelter behind a heavy coil of rope. The man started moving toward the very place where the poor sailor sat stunned and watching, but then the dark figure trailed off toward the hatchway of the rear cabins, where he disappeared. Olgaren pulled himself together and leaped across the deck to catch the man, but found the hatch sealed off. Locked from the outside as always. He was convinced that the devil himself was traveling with us, and he made the sign of the cross several times after finishing his confused tale.

Nobody was able to confirm Olgaren's story, and I calmed myself by thinking that the man must be suffering from some kind of superstitious hysteria. The uneasiness among the crew, however, now developed into a full-blown state of fear and confusion. I therefore ordered the ship searched from stern to bow.

We found nothing. The hold was the most likely place for a stowaway to hide, but it was easily inspected. We only carried the big boxes of black soil and mineral samples. There were no dark corners to hide in. We found nothing suspicious.

The tension among the crew slowly subsided, and once again everybody went quietly back to work. We were approaching the Gibraltar and sailed directly into a gale that lasted for three days and nights. There was no longer time for idle speculations concerning our night-walker. High spirits returned with the demanding labor of keeping the ship afloat in the rough weather. Even my guest soon began joining me at the dinner table.

Indeed he had recovered. He looked positively radiant and several years younger. He sought my company with an eagerness I hadn't expected, but I welcomed it happily. He completely captured my attention as he began unfolding the fascinating tale of his life and background.

It turned out that he, as I, was a born and bred Roumanian. He could trace his ancestors back to the thirteenth century, and his pride in his aristocratic lineage was obvious. I had never heard anyone speak so vividly about the history of our country as he told me of his ancestors' achievements among the upper aristocracy of medieval Roumania. Of course I could not boast of a similar lineage. My family have been simple farmers for generations, and their lives had passed without any of the dramatic changes or grandeur he seemed so familiar with. My abandoning the land to sail the seven seas was probably the greatest change they ever experienced.

You can imagine how I was swept away by the pleasant voice of my guest as he told me of heroic deeds and dramatic events in the remote past of my country. He finally revealed his name. It was Vlad, and he was the direct heir of a long line of crusaders — the Draculestis, holy knights of the Order of the Dragon, founded by the Roman church. These knights were nothing less than the bulwark of Europe. When the Ottoman Turks relentlessly stalked the European border for more than a century, the dragonfighters guarded the threshold of the Christian world. They were initiated in the name of the cross but at the same time the church wrapped the knights in the cloak of the dragon. They were expected to fight for good with the zeal of the devil.

The Order of the Dragon was a secret society whose number never exceeded twenty-four. Every one of them was recruited from the European aristocracy. Vlad's ancestor, who took the name

Dracul (the dragon) in token of his knighthood, fought for the sake of Christianity and for the safety of his country and kinsmen. He led a life in strict concordance with the dogmas of the Roman Catholic church, and his sons were raised and disciplined to live up to the convictions of their father.

But Dracul found himself in a particularly difficult position. On the one hand, he was principal guardian of the frontiers of Christianity. On the other, he was forced to maintain diplomatic relations with the superior forces of the Ottoman Turks, who kept their posts in the immediate vicinity of his country's border. He was appointed military governor of Transylvania but hoped to reestablish the right and privilege of the Wallachian throne that had once belonged to his ancestors.

I watched my guest as he told the story of ancient battles and political intrigues. It was as if he had taken part in everything himself. I was absolutely fascinated. The name Dracul is known by all Roumanians. This family of warriors and noblemen achieved great things for my country. They secured our borders and gained wealth and glory for their people. Their great deeds have never been forgotten, but neither has their cruelty. We also remember a regime of terror that has forever tainted the name of the Draculs. My guest was a

Dracul. Vlad had kept the epithet of his ancestors, Dracula, meaning "son of Dracul." All Dracul's descendants had used or inherited this name.

He abruptly ended his tale as it was getting late. He was exhausted and wanted to go to bed. He left me with a courteous bow.

The next morning, July 23, another man was missing. Again a victim of the lonely middle watch. His relief watch only found an empty deck, and a search revealed nothing. I reported another "freak accident" in the log.

We had by now passed the Gibraltar and were entering the Bay of Biscay. The weather had roughened again and I worried about my crew. If fear and hysteria broke out now, we would all be in great danger, as a storm was building. As captain I would be forced to punish severely anyone who caused a disturbance amongst the men by making wild accusations. Again we had searched the ship thoroughly and found nothing. There was nowhere for a murderous stowaway to hide. Unfortunately, this fact turned suspicions against my guest, but I found it completely absurd. Yes, the man was tall and well built, but he was also old and frail. Furthermore, he had been seasick in his cabin for days. I rejected the accusations vehemently and told my crew to hold their tongues.

You have to understand, I regarded the excitement of my men as the worst threat to our safety. I only knew how to handle problems I could see and understand. As captain it was my duty to ignore what seemed to be nothing but superstitious fantasies. I saw no reason to listen to the fears of my men.

My nightly conversations with Vlad provided a welcome opportunity to spend some pleasant hours forgetting about the lingering suspicion of something supernatural on board my ship. The tragic events of the past couple of days had not escaped my guest, and I felt that I ought to apologize for my crew's hasty and wrongful attacks on his honor. But Vlad did not take offense. As a man of the world he knew that the only stranger on board would most likely be regarded as an ill omen. He was never disturbed by the rising desperation around him. On the contrary, it seemed to amuse him. I could not help but frown at his lack of compassion. We had already suffered the loss of two good men on this journey, and I told him that I was deeply worried about the inexplicable accidents. How many men would be reported missing before we reached our destination?

His response was quick and strange. With a sinister look in his deep-set eyes he laid a heavy hand over mine and reminded me of my duties as a captain. The safety of the ship was my sole responsibility, he said, and if I did not bring my crew to their senses, mutiny and chaos would develop. However, he continued, if my authority could not be questioned, stability on the vessel would be secured immediately. It was time for me to take action.

I was only a simple sailor, not used to anything but carrying cargo from port to port. I had never in my life been challenged like this, and I loved my crew as if they were my own brothers.

I had not seen Vlad like this before. His look had an uncanny effect on my nerves, or was it his touch — burning like ice from the pole. For the first time I felt the power of the man, and strangely enough, it made me feel stronger, too. I was captain of the *Demeter* and it certainly was my duty to bring her safely to port. Only the unhindered propulsion of my ship mattered now.

Another week went by. The rough weather had turned into a full-blown gale. It felt as if we were trapped inside a devilish tornado with no means of escape. No one slept, and I no longer had time to entertain my guest as the steering of the ship took all the strength I had. In spite of our thorough search, we all felt the presence of an invisible enemy. The crew kept looking behind their backs. They felt doomed because there was nothing they could fight openly. They were on the verge of utter madness, but I succeeded in getting the men to concentrate on nothing but handling the ship. We were still in control.

Exhausted, I finally got a chance to withdraw to my cabin for a couple of hours and found Vlad waiting for me. He greeted me with his usual quaint politeness and bade me sit down with him for a while before turning in for a brief rest. Again I had to eat alone while he watched me. I asked him to continue the story of his ancestors. He nodded and started abruptly as if no time had elapsed since our previous session.

"Dracul received the insignia of the dragon in Nuremberg on the day of the birth of his second son — November 20, 1431. He accepted the knighthood of God clad in the golden necklace and cape of the order — green for the dragon's hue, worn over a blood-red coat in remembrance of the Christian martyrs.

"The golden necklace bore a symbolic engraving showing the victorious battle of Christ against the forces of darkness: a dragon hanging prostrate on a double cross — paws outstretched, jaw open, cleft back and tail curled around its head. The inscription was the motto of the order: '*O quam misericors est Deus — justus et pius.*' Oh, how God is merciful — just and faithful.

"From the moment Dracul took the oath of obedience, my family was dedicated to the service of God. For centuries we have been faithful to his promise. My life has from the very beginning been closely tied to the ways of my kin. My very existence is based on forces above the simple, one-dimensional ways of humanity. But do not misunderstand me. I only feel the presence of God through my pain. God exists, but without His counterpart in hell, there would be no divinity."

I had not expected Vlad's sudden leap to highly personal matters of faith. Until this evening he had insisted on telling me about an ancient line of blood, of aristocracy and religious orders. Now he suddenly saw fit to expose some dark burden on his mind, but with no explanation.

I did not understand him. The shadows around the man stayed impenetrable.

He continued, ignoring my startled face.

"Besides the responsibilities and rights of the crusader, Dracul finally regained his power as ruler of Wallachia. His lifelong battle to win back his lost land had ended. By serving God he had also managed to fulfill his worldly ambitions.

"Therefore another ceremony was arranged in the throne room of the fortress of Nuremberg. At last he had won his birthright. Thousands of people came to celebrate the newly appointed dragon knight and prince of Wallachia.

"A veiled woman in the imperial tribune

offered Dracul a priceless golden buckle as a token of her admiration. He accepted the trophy and kept it until the day he died. Dracul's second son would in time wear it in remembrance of his father."

My guest stopped. For a while he sat in silence with downcast eyes and his hands folded on the table in front of him. I waited respectfully for him to go on, but I could not help looking at him, and as I did, something strange happened. Vlad's silence seemed to draw me away from reality and into the realm of his mind.

Through a dreamy haze I saw the celebrating city of Nuremberg, every square and open space crowded with cheering people. Magicians and jesters were juggling and playing tricks. Singers and troubadours were chanting in foreign tongues.

In front of the Church of St. George a company of actors was about to begin a play. In the twilight eerie shadows were thrown onto the solid walls of the church, and bonfires tinted the heavy granite boulders a fiery crimson. The gothic structure of the pointed tower seemed the perfect setting for the players' ghostly pantomime.

A knight with the sign of the cross on his coat of armor steps out in front of a sad tableau — a beautiful woman lying in mourning across the body of her dead husband. She looks up. Her face is white and looks terrible. Her black eyes and red lips frighten me as she turns to the silent crowd.

The knight draws his sword. His face is hidden behind the hood of his cloak. Everyone is waiting for something to happen. It must be something about St. George slaying the dragon, but why is he hiding his face? And it's a woman in front of him, not a dragon.

The knight towers above the woman. She slowly rises, and the two figures face each other with the dead body lying between them. With a sudden movement the knight throws back the hood. It is not St. George! It is the ghastly face of death. The woman shows her teeth in a grin and throws herself against the edge of his sword. She pulls herself back and jumps forward once again before showing us her bloody wound. The crowd remains as silent as the miming actors. The blood is pouring down on the dead man. He is moving while the two others stand frozen in their positions. He rises and walks toward the audience. The blood has stained his naked chest and we see him drawing the sign of the cross on his skin. He speaks to us in a strange, hollow voice: "Blood is life. There is life in death. God has hidden behind the darkness of fear."

The commotion from the surrounding city replaces the deep silence of the church square. I turn around and see the waving flags and the shiny armor of the knights riding by as if they are flickering apparitions. The crowd parts and a single knight approaches the church. I see the Wallachian eagle on his coat of arms. He carries a large golden buckle on the tip of his lance. It is Dracul. I see him clearly as he stops on the square and dismounts. He is rather short and heavily built, giving a very powerful impression of raw force beneath the civilized appearance of the aristocratic crusader. He is completely still, and everything seems frozen in the moment while my vision gradually blurs.

I look up and find myself still sitting at the table with Vlad — my guest and entertainer.

It is very difficult for me to explain my state of mind. Behind his voice vividly describing people and events as remote and strange as a fairy tale, I sensed and actually saw this world of his. I saw what Vlad wanted me to see. He took me back in time and showed me how everything had happened.

I do not know how long we sat at the table — Vlad pressing my mind into his own reality, ignoring my silent questions. I knew it was late, for I heard the changing of the watch. It was the time of the cursed middle watch.

My guest apologized for having kept me up till

this hour and retired to his cabin. I went to my bunk to get some sleep. All night strange images kept passing in front of my eyes and left me tossing and turning in a cold sweat. It was a stormy night but the ship held her course, and I trusted my men. There was no obvious reason for my anxiety, but I kept throwing myself back and forth in the bunk in a fever of eerie dreams.

Ghostly pale women with red wolflike smiles came floating across a medieval tournament site where dying knights lay bleeding and moaning. The women threw themselves at the men and began licking their wounds. They kissed them with their crimson lips and bit them with their sharp white teeth. I saw Dracul, the champion, kneeling in front of the church. He was thanking God for the triumph. When he had finished his prayer he stood up and walked into the church through the huge portal that slowly opened as if unseen hands were pulling the heavy doors aside. He went to the altar with the moonlight flooding down through the gothic windows. The green cape hung from his shoulders in ripples. It seemed alive with its play of colors.

Lights and shadows were dancing in the cape's green fabric. The creases formed the outlines of sinister faces. They looked like horrible death-masks writhing in agonizing convulsions. The vision made my eyes burn and my body ache. I could not hold back any longer, and I screamed out in terror.

The sound of my voice seemed to stir up a cold gust of wind in the silent church. The cape was flapping around the shoulders on the motionless knight. New images slowly appeared in the green fabric, but this time they were full of beauty. There was my ship, the *Demeter*, riding the waves at full sail. The faded letters on her bow were now sharp and glittering as she sailed toward foreign coastlines.

Then the outline of Vlad's face replaced the image of my ship. His features were meticulously molded by the creases of the cape, and his unearthly look of hateful pride stunned me.

I knew at that moment that he had chosen me to carry out some hidden plan, and suddenly I felt lost. The shadows around the man had disappeared. He was young — ageless — and the stern dignity of the older man was replaced by a look so fierce and strong that it reminded me of long-forgotten nightmares. Dracul and Vlad resembled each other like brothers or father and son, but I clearly saw the difference between the two men. The difference was not physical but — how can I express it — spiritual in some way. The Knight of the Dragon, Dracul, was calm and at ease while Vlad, my guest, was restless and tormented. I felt as if I was looking in a mirror while seeing Vlad's face in front of me. Maybe he only reflected my anxiety.

I woke up, sweating and shivering, and as I opened my eyes I found Vlad sitting right beside me. His face was hidden by shadows but I saw the gleam in his eyes. He sat there looking at me in silence and I felt the storm rising outside. Then he spoke in a threatening voice. "Look to your ship, Captain! Your men are out of control. They have no strength left to handle her!"

It was time for the relief and I hurried on deck. Everything seemed all right and my men did not need any help or guidance. I wished I could ignore Vlad's unpleasant remark, but I found it hard to contain my anger. He had no business telling me how to run my ship, and he certainly was in no position to judge my crew's ability to hold her on course. He was my guest and therefore obliged to show me respect.

As the strange dreams lingered in my head, vague suspicions arose in my mind. Vlad was troubling me, but why? There was no reasonable explanation. The man had done nothing but vex me a little. He was just a passenger — my paying guest. How could he be connected with the tragedies we had experienced on this journey, let alone be responsible for them?

The storm was still blowing but not as hard as

before. I went to my cabin to get some rest. Still, I couldn't shake the feeling that something was wrong. I hesitated and went to see the mate.

I found him in a fit — something I had never expected to see. He told me that suddenly the ship would not respond to the rudder and he did not know why. Everything was in immaculate order, and the crew had thoroughly checked the ship's vital equipment several times. They found nothing out of order and still we were losing control.

Painfully aware of Vlad's warning, I ordered the men on deck. Every hand was needed now. We had to regain control of the ship. We toiled and exerted ourselves for hours, but nothing seemed to help. The only comfort was that the *Demeter* was keeping a steady course even though it wasn't our doing that kept her there. We shuddered at the thought of our complete helplessness. Something or someone else was steering our ship.

Panic took hold of every man on board. The *Demeter* was sailing on her own, and our efforts at the wheel were not having any effect. We dared not admit the futility of our efforts. We had to keep up the work in order to repress the rising terror of the unknown thing that was proving to be stronger than any of us.

Vlad kept to himself in his cabin while every man toiled away on deck. I wondered if he, too, felt the presence of some evil ghost leading us toward disaster and death. Did he sense our fear, or was he just watching us leap and jump at shadows? As the hours went by we resigned ourselves to our destiny. The ship seemed to be on a steady course and there was no danger of capsizing. I decided to keep up some appearance of normality and let my men take their usual shifts. But I ordered two men on deck during the middle watch. We had to avoid any more freak accidents.

On July 29 the mate offered to serve the middle watch alone. The men were exhausted. We could not keep up the double duty. They desperately needed to rest. I gave the mate my consent but in the morning we found the deck empty. We looked everywhere but he was gone.

I told the men to stay together so that nobody was left alone for even a couple of minutes. I went to my quarters to warn Vlad. He surely needed all the protection I could provide, and I decided to give him my gun for extra safety.

To my great astonishment I found him fast asleep. I tried to wake him but he did not even stir. I watched him in his sleep for a while. His face was calm and peaceful — a striking contrast to the worn and haggard faces of my men.

I stood there for what seemed a long time. He looked different. Vlad in his sleep looked several years younger than when I last talked to him. It was as if the years had been erased by magic. Even his hair had changed. It was no longer white but a dark shade of auburn.

I was completely baffled by this transformation, but I had to go back on deck to tend to more important matters. Here I stayed for the rest of the day, but I was disturbed by some vague danger connected with Vlad's presence on board. What had I done when I accepted his money back in Varna? Who was he?

I felt tormented by guilt, confusion and impotence. How could I save my ship when I did not know the cause of the horrible and mysterious tragedies haunting us?

We were approaching England, and we hoped and prayed for our rescue so close to this friendly coastline. The weather was fair and I allowed myself some hours of rest. At this point I felt it quite safe to leave everything in the hands of my men for a short while. They seemed calm and focused on their work.

It was dark when I woke up. Vlad was sitting at my table as usual. He had been watching me sleep, and it made me feel both peculiar and outraged. I no longer cared for the mental war going on between us. I felt like his puppet.

I rose and went to the table where I calmly sat

down to face him. I told him about the situation and reassured him that soon we would regain full control of the ship. I also told him of the loss of our mate. I did not really believe that he had slept through the storm without noticing the disturbance and panic on deck, but I gave him a complete account of what had happened. At least it made me feel in charge as captain. I apologized for not having informed him until now and tried desperately not to look directly into his piercing eyes. I was the captain and I could not let him get the better of me.

I had my say and handed him the gun. But instead of taking the weapon, he started talking to me in that dangerously smooth manner of his. I was forced to look up and let him lead the conversation. Again I was stunned by his appearance. He looked so young and strong, or perhaps it was my own fatigue that tricked my senses and made me see him like that. To me he seemed positively radiant from some inner force. It was as if he had undergone a metamorphosis during his sleep, while we aged under the pressure of our deadly fears.

He must have known what I was thinking and smiled at my confusion.

"I do not need your weapon," he finally said. "You do not know your enemy and, with all due respect, I question the effectiveness of this gun. We are now in English waters and no matter what happens this journey will soon end even though the captain of the vessel has stopped trying to navigate. We are still sailing directly toward our destination. Where is the danger?"

His tone of voice and the raised eyebrow provoked me. I felt slightly threatened but before I could respond he went on.

"Guard your men. Their safety is your responsibility. All this inexplicable loss of life has proven you a poor leader. You have not yet identified the danger lurking around us. You have not even tried. There is no stowaway on board and so the enemy must surely be one of us. Who is he? And who is to find out?"

Once again I had to endure his mockery. I painfully felt my own incompetence and could not find the words to reprove him. I was still completely baffled by the strange events taking place on my ship. I had never in my entire life experienced anything like this.

I was constantly haunted by the ghosts that possessed my mind, awake or asleep. I was beginning to doubt my mental faculties but I could do nothing but keep trying to see through all these foggy visions that obscured everything around me. How could I find a suitable answer to Vlad's provocations? How could I act when the cause of everything kept eluding me? I left the cabin without a word. Defeated.

On deck I was still captain. Still I could induce a sense of stability and order among the crew. I told them that I would stay on deck until we reached a safe harbor. I would only step out in order to conduct regular and thorough investigations of every corner of the ship. The date was July 30.

I did not know what we were up against, but I did not yet believe us to be completely helpless.

Later, I went below deck to make my rounds accompanied by one man. Suddenly we heard desperate cries from above. We rushed back on deck and found the cook in a state of bewilderment and panic. He had gone out to get some water and found the deck empty. We had lost both the helmsman and the look-out. They had been alone on deck for no more than a couple of minutes. Now we were only three men left besides Vlad in his cabin.

From now on we could only make feeble attempts to tend to the sails and rigging. We had to settle with that because we had no means of steering our ship. Still we kept hoping for rescue. We were passing the English Channel and we knew that now there was a strong possibility of meeting another ship, although the *Demeter* was shrouded in the thickest cloud of gray ever seen. We felt completely cut off from the rest of the world and our ship steered herself as if she were animated by some unearthly force. We were trapped inside this void and our only hope was to fight for our lives if we were given the chance to meet our adversary.

My men had settled their minds on certain doom and toiled stolidly with ropes and rigging. They were now way beyond fear, and their Russian fatalism enabled them to look straight into the eyes of death. I went below deck and searched every corner of the ship once again, knowing that there would be nothing to find. The large boxes seemed to have been moved but I assumed that the rough weather had made them slide a bit. Still, something kept nagging me. What if the men's initial suspicions were true? I had sailed with this crew for years and they had never before been prone to idle talk. Was Vlad causing these terrible accidents? Had he brought a curse on us simply by boarding our ship back in Varna? Was he our bird of ill omen? Five experienced sailors had vanished on this journey. Maybe they were struck by madness, but why?

I am Roumanian, and my country has many secrets. They are not all of this world, and if God wasn't holding our course in this impenetrable fog, then someone else was. The fact that Vlad was my compatriot made me shudder. I started to acknowledge what I subconsciously had known all along. I knew who he was, and what he was! But this did not do any good now. If I was right, resistance would be futile.

At this point I started to hope that I was going mad. That madness would save me from terrors to come.

On August 2, around midnight, a scream from deck woke me up. Exhaustion had forced me to my bunk for a couple of minutes, but now I leaped up as if the devil was pinching my back. I rushed outside but couldn't see anything in the fog, and I was very nearly run over by my cook. The poor simple-minded man had been on deck with my other man — each on the look-out on opposite sides of the ship. He had searched everywhere after hearing the scream but to no avail. The deck seemed empty except for the two of us. We called out but got no answer. The wheel was abandoned.

We were now certain that nothing could save us. Something had taken my crew, and it would continue to attack until we were all gone. We had no choice but to face this terror before it crept up behind us, even though the mere thought of facing it was abominable. The cook, my last friend and companion, no longer bore the slightest resemblance to the man he used to be. He was raving like a madman, and when I tried to calm him down he pushed me aside and ran below to the hold. I heard him rummaging and knew that he was trying to move the heavy boxes of soil. I let him do it because the exertions would save him from a total breakdown.

A couple of minutes went by. I was standing on deck trying to catch sight of either a buoy or a landmark when I heard a yell. I turned and saw the poor man running toward me with his hair standing on end.

"He is here!" he screamed. "Now I know who your guest really is. There is no hope for us and you'd better follow me!" With these words he rushed to the bulwark and jumped overboard. He was gone before I could make any attempt to save him.

I was alone on my ship. With Vlad. The last man of my crew had made no mistake about my guest. He was terror incarnate. The cook had surely opened the boxes below, and what he had found had made him throw himself into the ocean. I knew now that they contained more than scientific samples. The boxes of Roumanian soil were a vital part of Vlad's survival abroad. Anyone who touched it would immediately feel the abomination in it.

Had I not been captain of the ship I would have jumped overboard as well. The silence around me, emphasized by the creaking of my lost ship, was unbearable. I was his hostage in a foggy No Man's Land. Awaiting the final unveiling of his devilish game, I stayed on deck all night long. I did not possess the courage to make a move.

I knew what was in store for me — one last humiliating meeting with the man I had willingly invited on board. He was superior to me. Neither cunning nor brute force could match his strength. I had already seen this demonstrated at the cost of many lives.

But I couldn't just capitulate. I still had a chance to save my honor as captain of the *Demeter*. So I stayed and waited.

The dim light of dawn came. I was almost certain that my life would be over by nightfall. I was weak from the cold and the strain of days of fear and struggle. I had no strength left, but a lingering hope of salvation kept me going. I decided to tie myself to the wheel and let the little cross hanging around my neck show. If he came to get me, the cross would at least protect my Christian soul.

Finally the dark fell around me. I was barely conscious after so many hours tied to the wheel. My last report in the log was made on August 2. We were sailing along the east coast of England as far as I could tell. The fog was still enclosing the ship. The *Demeter* was caught in a dank grip and sailed her course directed by the force of a strong and sinister mind.

At this point I no longer trusted my senses. The date must have been August 4. I expected this day to be my last ... Nosferatu!

LUCIA'S DIARY

June 10, 1994

Dear Grandfather,

Yesterday I was sitting in the park reading the first bit of Maresciu's tale. It was the first really hot day of the summer, but the story almost made me feel the cold and clammy fog lingering around the ghostly ship. I certainly understand yours, and great-grandfather's, fascination with the old sailor's account of his last journey. It is a genuine ghost story. Nosferatu means vampire, am I right? I looked it up. *Chronicles of the Vampire* says that the vampire, perfectly resembling a human being, is a figment of our wishful dreams about eternal youth and superhuman strength. We like to think that he can offer these things if we accept his nocturnal existence. That indeed we can, if we can bear the thought of being what he is, challenge time and space. He holds our imagination and our dreams in a firm grip, but only to lead us on to nightmares and despair! Well, that's what the book says.

I remember the vampires of my childhood. They appeared in the old black-and-white late-night movies. Elegant creatures, always in full evening clothes and even wearing capes of black silk. They were always accompanied by eerie music and beautiful, pale women. And crosses and coffins!

But who is Vlad? A vampire? How can I accept that? The vampire is a grotesque fantasy figure who represents our hidden and impossible desires. Is that all there is to the tragic events described by Maresciu? Something else must have happened.

I know that the crew disappeared one by one — except Maresciu himself, of course, and maybe the person he refers to as Vlad. Was he real? Are these facts? It all seems so farfetched. Fascinating, I admit, but not very likely. It's as if the storyteller is weaving tiny threads of his own imagination into the account of what happened on the *Demeter*. But who am I to decide whether it is true or not? Vlad is more than just a reflection of the captain's fear and weakness. I read Maresciu's story and I can actually picture this strange passenger on the ship. He seems present in every word.

But I have only begun reading. I must concentrate and let myself sink deeper into Maresciu's tale.

Arthur came by last night. I was feeding

Delifrena her daily ration of insects. Wille has made an arrangement with his fellow researchers at the biological laboratory. I am free to go there and get all the supplies for Delifrena that I need.

Arthur disapproves of Delifrena. I have no idea why. She is an extremely beautiful specimen of the family *Lycosa saccata* — the wolf spider. Even the name has a poetic sound to it. But Arthur finds spiders revolting. He would never admit it, of course, but I have told him that it is all right. Delifrena is Wille's pet, not mine, though I must admit that she has a certain charm. All she wants is her little insects, and when I give them to her she swiftly prepares her dinner. I have grown quite fond of her. She is a good listener and a joy to watch while she is nestling in her glass cage. She is simply good company.

Arthur wants to travel for the next couple of months. He wants me to go along but I have told him that I have to stay here with Delifrena. It seems very hard for him to understand why I prefer to stay here on my own. Still, I'm determined to let him go without me. I'll really be better off here in Wille's dusty maze of an apartment. I need some time on my own. Lately it has felt like a nightmare attending the classes in the dissection room. It has been increasingly hard to concentrate on the assignments, let alone listen to the professors. I'm sick of it. Jars of body parts preserved in formaldehyde. A limb so well kept that every little hair is still there. Organs slightly yellowed by the liquid they are floating in, but otherwise perfect.

It seems to me that we're living in a world of institutes and laboratories where everything is organized and cataloged by the strictest rules — torsos, limbs, heads. We donate our bodies to science and thereby submit to the great system of immaculate order and neatness. We aren't concerned with the individual. We only want perfect specimens representing the unique functionalism of the human body. We all share the potential of our race, but still we hobble along without the slightest concern for our fellow men.

But not to worry. The chaos of differences in life is put to an end in death. In death we are all the same. The medical world looks upon the body as a common denominator in order to treat the individual despite all our differences. Is it an illusion shared by us all? Can we accept chaos and disorder in nature? Can we accept that nature does not repeat itself in creation but on the contrary renews itself constantly and thereby allows the impossible to exist?

Night came. I only vaguely perceived the shift from grayness to darkness. I was half dead from hunger, cold and fatigue, and I could do nothing but wait. The hatchway was open but I chose to look at the stars. They gave me some consolation. I prayed to God for strength in my last moments. I could not allow myself to leave my ship now that the end was so near. Everything around me was shrouded in darkness, and I fell into a blessed state of numbness.

I regained my senses later in the night. I no longer felt the cold, nor did I feel my hunger and exhaustion. I was certain that I had died and been taken prisoner in his world. I have always known about the afterlife of the lost souls. Where I come from necuratul — you Westerners are probably more familiar with the term nosferatu — feeds on our fears. We know about their nocturnal existence, but we never cross the line between their world and ours. We know their secrets — centuries of tragic experience have taught us about them — but our knowledge is never enough. Our strength and our God can not prevail when we try to fight their dark force. Necuratul is, and always will be, part of God's creation and therefore invincible.

I saw him. He was standing as a shadow in the

faint light of the lantern. His face was turned away from me and he seemed absorbed in thoughts of his own. I was still feeling numb and strangely calm. I looked at the towering figure and waited for him to turn and face me. No thoughts went through my mind at that moment. I was completely focused on the man who held me captive on my own ship. The rest of the world no longer existed.

"Now you see me, my friend." He spoke, as always, in our shared native tongue. "For the time being I have lent you strength and immunity. You no longer feel any pain and you are ready to understand who I am."

He turned and took the lantern from the hook. Now I saw his face clearly. It was the Vlad from my dreams. He looked young, about thirty-five years old. I stared into his deep-set green eyes. The expression was grim. The lantern in his left hand lit up his face from below. He looked haggard and sallow. I recognized the high, prominent cheek-bones, the jutting chin and the long, aquiline nose, but the aristocratic refinement of the older man's visage was gone. Instead the features of the younger Vlad were tainted with cruelty and arrogance. His hair had become a dark, auburn color as were his moustache and his eyebrows. The tightly sealed lower lip, which was visible below his heavy moustache, was as red as blood.

This moment seemed frozen in time, lasting an eternity. The sight of the figure in front of me burned itself into my mind. I felt as if I was forced to perceive and acknowledge the complete depth of his being, and I sensed, even more strongly than in my dreams, the battles and intrigues of past centuries. I sensed a chaos of sadistic cruelty hidden in his soul.

He was dressed as a boyar, the ancient aristocracy of my country. Faded splendor of the Middle Ages. A wide collar of sable and gold brocade covered his purple mantle, which was closed with three large gold buttons. He wore close-fitting headgear of red silk with nine rows of pearls at the brim and a star-shaped brooch of topaz in the center holding a large cluster of glittering jewels. I saw the heavy gold buckle fitted inside the rim of the mantle. Only Dracul's son could wear that prize. He was also wearing black boots and black leather pants that were wet and glittery from the salt water and the cold sea fog around us.

"You see me, and you are ready to listen," he repeated. "Your futile attempt to call upon the protection of your God will not work here. I am the captain of the *Demeter* and you are my slave." With a swift and brutal movement he tore the necklace with the cross from my neck and tossed it into the sea.

"You know me for what I truly am. We are countrymen and I have chosen to spare your life because of this. Only you can fully comprehend my story. The rest of your crew have given their lives so that I could regain my youth and strength.

"I have waited for this moment. We are now sailing along the coastline of England — my destination. But before I invade this great land with its teeming population, I want to tell my story to someone who will not let it be forgotten. I want to secure my place here by your voice repeating my story. I know that I will be challenged in this new world. Forces will try to destroy me. Westerners are not as easy to cow as the frightened and miserable people of my homeland. But I will overcome every obstacle and win my battle with the Western world. I will find my bride here, and we will crowd the world with my children — my slaves."

He was right. I knew him well, and had indeed known him for as long as I could remember. My dreams were not mere ravings. They were not even forced upon me by Vlad's hypnotic powers. They were stored deep in my mind — infantile knowledge of myths and legends. His name is known and feared by every Roumanian. He is part of our history and our nightmares. His regime of terror has held my people in a tight grip ever since his death in 1476. His body was never found. Necuratul — the devil — is his true name.

He continued. "I am Vlad Dracula, the second son of Vlad Dracul and Princess Cneajna. I am prince of Wallachia and Transylvania. I see that you have tied yourself to the wheel, and I find that a most suitable position for you, my friend. You may stay there until I have finished my story.

"In my part of the world I am famous, as you well know. As long as I haunt people's minds and live in every nightmare, my power is undiminished. But in England and the Western world my name represents only a vague caricature. A mere shadow fit to scare children. Only a few know my name and even fewer understand who I am. But respect and fear will prevail in the West. I will not cease to attack, and who can find the strength to stop me? So listen to me, you weakling! How do you like dangling on a wheel that will only bend to my will? The fog will not disappear until I have had my say."

He bent over and looked me straight in the eyes. His face was only inches from mine and the stench of his breath made me feel faint. He noticed it and grabbed me by my hair. His staring eyes held me in agony.

"You know me but only from legend and old wives' tales. You know necuratul, but you and the other peasants, crossing themselves and locking their doors at sundown, do not recall what my kin did for Roumania."

His soft voice made my hair stand on end. The hatred and fury felt like electricity in the air between us.

Icy gusts of wind swept the deck. My limbs were flapping around me like the limbs of a rag doll as I lay by the wheel. My eyes were completely focused on the figure in front of me. He had put down the lantern on a coil of rope and began pacing back and forth. The fog floating like smoke in the air between us, the faint flickering light of the lantern and the lonely, creaking sounds of my ship made the scenery around us seem unreal and ghostly. It felt as if we were enclosed by solid walls, in a room completely dominated by the presence of Dracula. I was breathing only at his will but still I felt calm and numb, in a paralysis inflicted on me by an evil force I could not fight.

At least he was not going to kill me. My life had a certain value to him. I was going to listen and when he had finished ... I did not even dare to think about what would happen then.

He stooped again and looked at me.

"You are a sailor. You know the laws of nature. You have learned to travel safely by sea because you know the rules and conditions of this element.

Your knowledge is your survival. But I tell you that I am not subject to any rules of this world. Look at your ship — at what was once your ship, I should say. Look at the fog and the sea around us. I control these forces. I can tame the waves or make them rise in front of us as solid walls. The current will take us wherever I want, and I can terminate your life in a second."

He stood up and started pacing the deck again. Vlad now continued his story. And I listened.

MARESCIU'S TALE

"I was raised in the fortress of Tirgoviste, a small and quite humble residence by the standards of the time but tactically well situated in the mountains of the southern border. It was absolutely impregnable and the Ottoman Turks seldom attempted an attack. Here I lived from my fifth to my eleventh year. During this time my brothers and I were taught the skills of knighthood. At the age of five I was already a skilled horseman. I was also taught the arts of fencing and archery, and I learned to swim and wrestle. My intellect was sharpened by the best tutors, who gave me thorough lessons in philosophy and political knowledge. I learned many languages and how to conduct myself at court.

"My nurses and servants treated me with due respect. They acted upon my every whim. I did not see my father much. He trusted that the obedience of the women would suffice to make his sons act like princes. He saw to it that only the most humble and fearful girls were hired to wait on us. It was made perfectly clear to every servant in our quarters that we were in command. We could have any of them rewarded or executed as we saw fit.

"I particularly remember one episode of my childhood, when a servant girl tried to disobey my demands. My brother and I had made up a game she did not care for. I must have been about ten years old.

"Our bedroom windows faced the inner courtyard where criminals were executed from time to time. Comfortably seated on the windowsill, my brothers and I were able to watch the scenery of death. Now I wanted to get a closer look at it.

"Preparations for an execution always included digging a grave for the body by the north side of the rampart. The earth was unconsecrated, and hundreds of criminals were buried there. I wanted to know the hidden darkness of these graves. The secrets of restless souls and the utter damnation of their confinement below ground had occupied my thoughts for quite some time. You see, I had noticed the fear and terror in the eyes of the soldiers guarding the rampart. At night they never came near the north side. They only kept watch from the towers of the other wings. Ghastly tales of apparitions and walking dead men circulated among the girls and women.

"Valpurga, a pale and thin girl from the laundry house, was known to be clairvoyant, and naturally I chose her to assist me in my quest for knowledge. I wanted an agent put down in the soil of the lost souls. A grave had been prepared for a hanging at daybreak, and I wanted her to get down there, lie under a thin cover of earth, and wait for the dead man's body. My brother Radu had made a construction of tubes and pointed poles to hold it so that the girl would be able to breathe. If she died of suffocation nothing would be gained. She had to survive down there for at least twenty-four hours so that she could give us a complete account of what happened to the dead man after midnight.

"Well, we went to her room at night and told her to follow us. We took her outside, creeping through an old tunnel we had recently discovered, and went to the rampart. At this point she started crying and begging. We had, of course, expected some resistance, but we warned her of the consequences if she disobeyed us. So she reluctantly started lowering herself into the grave, not yet knowing the full extent of our plans.

"Just as I was going to give the girl her instructions, she had a seizure and fell down foaming and scratching. Her eyes were rolling blindly and her body was twisted in cramps. We could do nothing but wait. The seizure lasted for minutes and left her lying in a deathlike swoon. My cowardly brother ran away in terror and left me alone with the girl. He was still holding onto the tubes, so she had escaped my first experiment, but I refused to give up. The other world felt close enough to reach if I only made an effort.

"An impulse altered my life completely. I jumped into the grave and began covering the still girl with earth. She woke up when the dank soil fell on her face and looked at me with eyes so terrified that I knew I was doing the right thing. She screamed piercingly, but I quickly stopped her by thrusting one of the pointed poles into her chest. My original plan — of having a living agent in the ground — was abandoned. Now I knew that the death of the girl would produce even more than my former intentions. I felt the living darkness around me, an evil force in the abyss calling my name. I would not let anything stop me now.

"The girl squirmed under the pole and bubbles of blood appeared in her open mouth. I dug the pole deeper into her body and twisted it a couple of times until I felt it go right through her. Everything went completely still, but only for a second. Then I heard a roaring rush above me. It felt as if giant birds were sweeping past.

"It was a victory. I had crossed the line between worlds without yet knowing the nature of this new and dark place. Invisible beings were whirling around me, and I was pushed down on my back. I got up and still these phantoms were circling around me at incredible speed. The sound was breathtaking. It was eerie and beautiful music. Faster and faster they went. It was as if they were trying to capture my mind and make me feel the secrets of their existence. It was an ecstatic feeling.

"The sound grew louder until it was absolutely earsplitting. I felt some sort of climax coming. I waited and kept listening to the sound of beating and pounding in my bleeding ears.

"Then it happened! The frenzy around me stopped for one second, and renewed itself with double force the next. It went right through me. I was carried up and floated in midair above the grave below. It felt as if my body had been torn in two but there was no pain.

"At that moment I was allowed a glimpse of this other world. I had felt its presence before, but now I clearly saw it for a few seconds. It would no longer be a distant haze to me. It was real and I could be allowed to enter it some day. This was a gift for the one who dared receive it. I had sought it, and this was my reward. I both saw and felt this universe full of immense powers and unlimited possibilities, and I knew that I had been living in a prison of limitations.

"The dark sphere was completely devoid of the civilization that we know. The bidding of Christianity did not exist. Charity, ethics, faith in God — none of this had any meaning in the darkness. No love. Only the unlimited force of ruthless, evil ambition.

"I knew this to be my destiny.

"I was only a child at the time. I was neither strong enough nor capable of understanding the full meaning of my experience. Only years and many sufferings later would I fully recognize what I had found and who I really was."

LUCIA'S DIARY

June 11, 1994

It's sickening! Vlad Dracula, a terrible ghost from an age of barbarism and bloodshed, has tainted the lives of my grandfather and great-grandfather. How many more? This ghost, this Dracula, was not just a figment of a sailor's imagination. He was there, and maybe he is still around somewhere. I feel him. But why was it so important to reveal these horrors? To what purpose?

How ironic! The world was told nothing about him. Maresciu's log was silent and these documents have been hidden. Only my family has read them.

June 12, 1994

Dear Grandfather,

I'm reading Vlad's tale now. Bit by bit. You were right. It is not just some funny old ghost story. I had certainly not expected this. A medieval prince is speaking to me from these old pages. And who would have believed that I would become absorbed in events so strange and unbelievable.

Last night I was stunned by what I had just read. I could hardly fall asleep. I kept telling myself that it was just a fantasy concocted by a lunatic sailor, but in the back of my mind I knew that I had been reading the true story of what happened on the *Demeter*.

Vlad Dracula was really there.

MARESCIU'S TALE

It was horrifying listening to Dracula's story. His words brought back memories of legends and old tales of terror.

Even as a child, Dracula was an outsider. A

deviant human being. He was then what he is today. An outsider without any real bonds to the natural world. A freak who chose to seek his own truth beyond the limits of the human order.

He was destined to be the tenth scholar of the Scholomance, the school of the devil lying somewhere in the heart of the mountains. This is the place to learn the secrets of nature, the language of animals and all magic spells. Only ten scholars are admitted at a time, and when the course of learning has expired, only nine are released. The tenth scholar is held back as the devil's payment and mounted on an ismeju, a dragon. From this moment on he is the devil's assistant in every evil project. The storytellers of my childhood may not have been entirely wrong when they told me this tale. Obviously Dracula had found some dark magic to make him live forever.

He was standing in front of me looking like a massive tower against the grayish-white world of fog surrounding us.

"I woke up and returned to the reality I had left for a moment and fell down on top of the girl in the criminal's grave. She was still but smiling an eternal smile of blood. She was the guardian of this passage. In time I would follow her and reach the other side where my prize would be waiting for me. The pole through her body was standing erect, a symbol of my victory over human weakness.

"It was daybreak by now and I quickly covered the dead girl with dirt. She would certainly not be detected by the soldiers and gravediggers. They would hastily dispose of their burden and hurry back to the safety of the fortress. No one stayed by these unholy graves longer than absolutely necessary. The place therefore belonged to me. I was the only one who knew what was there.

"I returned to the fortress and went back to my room. I was just in time to see the execution in the yard below.

"I never told anyone about my experience at the northern rampart. It was clear to me that there was still much more to be revealed. I longed to see this wonderful world beyond the grave, and instinctively I knew that everything would belong to me one day. I only had to wait.

"As it happened, my life in Tirgoviste was coming to an end.

"My father's position as sworn defender of Christian territory in a country surrounded by Ottoman powers was demanding. He used all his political cunning and tactical skill to survive. You see, Vlad Dracul was a man of reason. He was never tempted to risk his army in hasty demonstrations of force, as he knew how fatal that could be. He always waited for the right time to strike, and only if negotiations had proven futile."

Dracula fell silent for a couple of minutes. His silence immediately took me back to the cold deck of the *Demeter*. The wheel was slowly turning back and forth, and I let my useless body follow the idle movements. Only my consciousness was alive and alert. I was held in the grip of Dracula's tale, and as he stood there, absorbed in thoughts of his own, I felt the breathless anxiety of things to come. My eyes fell on his profile and I noticed a peculiar twitch of his lower lip. It gave his entire face an awful, drawn expression of complete lunacy. I wondered whether this madness was the cost of eternal life. Had Dracula been mad all along? I doubted it. In his time cruelty and obsession were a common mark of nobility. His nature would certainly be regarded as utter madness in our time. But this strange twitch ... I knew that the legends indicated that he was a sick man, but they also indicated that this sickness was due to some connection with the forces of darkness. Could this supernatural being be just plain humanly mad?

Of course not. I was looking at a living dead on his quest for new territories. Speculations about his sanity were my own madness.

But my terror was subdued now. I had begun to listen to his story. The voice, the rapid changes of focus and the sudden outbursts of anger — everything about him held me spellbound. I heard about political maneuvers and bloody battles in the county he once ruled. I learned about the terms of existence in a country torn between Christianity and Islam. And gradually I lost sight of the terrifying monster and, beyond the limits of reason, saw the man behind the ghost. His childhood story was nauseating, I admit that. It turned my stomach to hear what he had done, but now I eagerly waited for him to continue the story.

The little I knew of the real-life Dracula was from a bit of military history and tales of the internal affairs of court and country. Some of it revealed a lust for power and a debauched lifestyle, but other parts of our history told of a prince who knew how to defend his country and keep up a wealthy community.

Our country was buried in the dark Middle Ages while Western Europe celebrated the new age of light and wisdom. The newborn humanity of the West, the glory of the Renaissance, did not affect the East. Too much was at stake should the deadly fear of a cruel God come to an end. The Roumanian people were yoked by the church and the unlimited power of the rulers. They did not even believe in the existence of another world order. The people of the West learned and prospered from the benefits of science and education while my people were living in the shadow of aristocracy and religion. God was not the ally of peasants and poor people, but He was the only bulwark against the threat of the Ottoman crescent.

I would listen to every word Dracula had to say. The fear of what would happen next had vanished. It did not matter right now. I wanted to know what life had been like in the Dark Ages.

The voice of Dracula interrupted my thoughts.

"My father was utterly wrong. His political maneuvers backfired and it nearly cost us our lives. Wallachia was vulnerable and it was necessary to reach a ceasefire agreement with the Ottoman Empire. In 1442 the Ottoman army had won full control over the river Danube, including two important fortresses. Nobody had been able to stop their hostile progression. My father was painfully aware of his dangerous position. The Western powers were pushing the notion of resuming Crusades and holy wars. They wanted to crush the Ottoman aggression once and for all. Dracul, of course, was a sworn Dragon knight, but how could he risk a war against the Ottoman Empire? He knew that no support for his army could be expected, as the neighboring countries of Hungary and Poland were both shaken by internal power struggles.

"My father found himself in a difficult dilemma. His position depended on his relationship to the church and the Western world. He had powerful rivals to the throne and they would not hesitate to challenge his right to rule should he fail to defend Christianity against the Turks. At the same time Sultan Murad II had spies everywhere in my father's court to make sure the ceasefire agreement at the border was kept. Should Dracul decide to act against the Turks, Murad would be the first to know. War would break out between Wallachia and the Ottoman Empire, and Dracul's army would never survive a battle against the Turkish forces.

"He made his choice, hoping to survive this dilemma by taking both sides. Secretly he let the Turks cross the border and continue toward Transylvania. He knew that beyond the great forests waited a considerable force of armed soldiers. They totally outnumbered the unsuspecting Turks, but Dracul kept this knowledge to himself.

"Of course Murad saw through my father's attempt to please two parties. So he acted without hesitation to secure Dracul's unconditional support in the future.

"In the spring a Turkish delegation summoned my father to a meeting in Gallipoli. My father had no choice but to go, but he trusted that his understanding with the sultan would secure his course on Ottoman territory. He appointed my brother, Mircea, constituent ruler during his absence and ordered my younger brother, Radu, and myself to follow him on his journey. I was eleven years old at the time. Radu was four years younger.

"When we arrived at the gates of Gallipoli, we were met by a battalion of soldiers. They immediately put my father in chains and took him away. My brother and I were led to a group of horsemen. We traveled through deserted hillsides for days and finally we reached the fortress of Egrigöz somewhere in the distant mountains of Anatolia. We knew nothing of what had happened to our father and felt certain that we would suffer torture and unspeakable horrors in the Turkish dungeons."

Dracula stood silent for a while, remembering his captivity in the land of the enemy. His eyes were flaring with a reddish glow.

Was he real or just a figment of my imagination? Was he dead or alive? Maybe we were both dead and caught in a ghastly No Man's World on the deck of my ship.

I clung to the promise that we would in time reach England. Our journey was suspended for the time being, but as soon as he had told me his tale we would return to the world of the living. Then I would be his voice. He feared oblivion more than anything, I knew that by now. If I managed to keep my sanity there was still hope for my salvation.

Once again his voice started speaking and emptied my mind of anything else.

"We did not understand the language of our guards, and even though the land around us looked like the mountains of home, we knew that we were being taken farther and farther away from everything familiar to us. We had entered a world we did not know. The world of Islam.

"We were treated fairly, but I had on several occasions heard my father's spies talk about the Turkish way of handling their hostages. At any moment they might decide to make an example of either one of us. At any moment we could have our heads severed from our bodies.

"We were led to some private quarters in the western wing. The view from the narrow peepholes was beautiful and depressing. We found ourselves completely isolated. There was nothing but deserted mountains around us. Even the sunset seemed more distant than ever. But the Turks treated us with respect, and we never suffered from cold, hunger or thirst. As they did not speak our tongue and we could not understand theirs, it was impossible to communicate. We had to live with the possibility of our father's death, as well as not knowing what would eventually happen to us.

"I learned about patience in Egrigöz. I learned how to wait and keep my mind on revenge without falling apart in anger and despair. One day Murad would answer to me and the score would be settled.

"The monotony was almost unbearable. Our only view was the mountains. We were completely cut off from the rest of the fortress. If we had at least been able to see what was going on in the courtyard, we could have amused ourselves watching the guards and the other prisoners. But we were left to our own company. The only other person we ever saw was the soldier who guarded our door and brought us what we needed twice a day.

"For three months we lived in isolation, ignorant and bored. When finally we were led out into the courtyard, our horses were brought out. We were leaving with the same soldiers who had brought us here but we had no way of knowing where they were taking us.

"We traveled for weeks. I still remember the heat, the dust, the exhaustion and the strange tongue of our guardians. They kept us under close watch but we were never harmed. They shared their meals with us and slept by the same fire at night. Still, no one ever talked to us. We were prisoners being transported from one jail to another.

"Finally we reached our destination — Adrianople, the capital city. Murad's stronghold. We were led directly to court and for the first time in months we faced a man with whom we could communicate. His name was Castriota, boyar and prisoner in Murad's palace. He welcomed us and led us through halls of immense riches and luxury. A bath had been made ready for us, and our clothes were replaced by costly Turkish robes. Rested and refreshed, we sat down with Castriota, who told us everything we needed to know.

"We could consider ourselves the prisoners of the sultan. He intended to keep us here for a very long time, if not forever. My father had been released shortly after our departure from Gallipoli and Murad's soldiers had escorted him all the way home to make sure that he made no attempt to follow us. Murad had spared his and our lives on the strictest conditions. Dracul could return home after having sworn on both the Bible and the Koran not to take further actions against the Ottoman Empire.

"My brother and I were Murad's guarantee of Dracul's future loyalty. We would be treated according to our rank and importance. There was no doubt that Murad intended to keep us here for many years to come. We soon learned that hundreds of "guests" like us were staying in the palace.

Children in a golden cage due to their fathers' deceit or lack of cooperation. The Ottoman education was also Murad's refined method of modeling the sons of his allies and thus securing future bonds with the European rulers. These boys sooner or later would be released to claim their land and thrones after the many years of Ottoman schooling. That is, if they behaved and their fathers did likewise.

"So it seemed that my brother Radu and I could look forward to quite a comfortable life at the Ottoman court, as long as Dracul kept his promises. We would benefit from the best teachers and an education similar to that of the sultan's own sons. My upbringing was from that moment guided strictly according to the highly refined and completely alien culture of the Ottoman Empire. Priests, philosophers and mathematicians — all names that were famous and respected in the West — gave us daily lessons and each one of them had the right to flog their pupils should we fail to learn the complicated wisdom of their science. Before long we had mastered the language without difficulty and we were free to go almost everywhere within the palace walls. Every facility was at our disposal as long as we respected the conditions of our relative freedom.

"My brother quickly settled in and enjoyed the

luxurious surroundings. He was a gentle and coquettish boy, well liked by everyone. He looked like a girl with his beautiful features and long wavy hair, and in no time he was the pet of the entire harem, not to mention a great many of the noblemen at court. Even the sultan's son, Mehmed, favored young Radu by showing him unsavory and unrestrained affection. Radu quickly gave in to the lovesick Mehmed and gained a privileged position as a royal mascot and bed companion.

"It revolted me. I did not possess Radu's beauty nor did anyone take particular interest in me, as I was considered particularly uncongenial. It was a great relief because it enabled me to wander about between lessons without being noticed. During lessons, however, the teachers took a special, nasty interest in chastising me to put an end to my rebellious behavior. Thus, like Radu, I had to swallow my pride and take on different manners in order to survive. I would surely have been beaten to death had I kept taunting my tutors. I resigned myself to it for the time being, I kept my temper and followed their orders, but I never let them forget that I was Dracula, son of Dracul, and somehow it made them respect me. Of course, I never enjoyed any special privileges as my brother did. On the contrary, my constant, passive resistance cost me regular punishment. But I decided that I never wanted to be anything more than their royal hostage.

"Still, I made use of every hour in Murad's palace. I read eagerly and listened to every word of education from my tutors, as I knew that knowledge was a benefit that would last me a lifetime.

"I looked on the Turkish culture as a way to expand my view of the world and I merely frowned at whatever revolted me. I never forgot what I had promised myself — to leave this place wiser and capable of understanding the Ottoman logic. If I succeeded I would also have achieved the most difficult virtues, namely patience and an ability to stay calm no matter what happened. You see, I was constantly aware that Murad could kill me whenever he pleased. I never doubted that he would act if the slightest irregularity concerning Dracul's conduct should be reported.

"Everywhere around me promiscuity flourished. Decadence and perversion held even the strongest and most important courtiers in a grip. Only a few could resist the distractions offered by the harem as well as the male servants. I witnessed unspeakable perversions from my hidden positions at doors standing slightly ajar or by the window. In my early childhood I had seen similar happenings in the hidden corners and private bedrooms of my father's castle, but I had not fully understood the implications of these things until now. I learned that it was better to refrain from them in order to stay calm and take advantage of the sad lot of passion slaves.

"On my fifteenth birthday something happened that changed my view of the world. Castriota, the fellow prisoner who had welcomed us to the castle, had for some time shown a great deal of interest in me. He even addressed me as his equal in spite of the fact that he enjoyed the trust and confidence of the sultan himself. Castriota was a highly talented and very intelligent aristocrat. His political sense and diplomatic skills had secured his position among the leaders even during imprisonment. He had worked hard to get there, but now, years after being taken prisoner by Murad's soldiers, he was an important counsellor at court.

"On my birthday I stepped forward and demanded permission to send and receive messages from my father. So far I had been kept ignorant of events going on outside Murad's palace. I knew absolutely nothing of the situation in Wallachia. How could I prepare for a life outside this prison if every bit of information was kept from me? You must understand that I frantically clung to the notion of my future release. But as I knew nothing of my father's conduct, I had no chance of knowing whether my freedom would ever be granted. Having reached the age of fifteen I felt entitled to a certain number of rights. I declared that if my wish was not granted they would have to lock me up in a dungeon to keep me from trying to escape. I would no longer stay passive in this golden cage.

"This bravado was very dangerous. However, I felt that it was time to risk it. I wanted a settlement with my guardians. I was not going to let them humiliate me anymore.

"I was very lucky that Castriota was present during my rebellion. He managed to calm down my agitated teachers and suggested that I accompany him on a ride outside the palace walls. This request was very bold and I expected it to be turned down immediately, but to my utter surprise it was granted. I was dismissed for the rest of the day and entrusted to the care of my rescuer.

"So far we had only exchanged a couple of formal remarks, and I considered Castriota a mere puppet of the sultan. He could go anywhere he wanted inside and outside the palace, and he was highly valued at court. He simply had to be some sort of a traitor. Therefore I had never felt any urge to engage in conversation with him even though his native country, Serbia, shared a border with mine. He seemed too well established in the dealings of the enemy. The fact that I was allowed to follow him outside the palace convinced me that he could be nothing but a spy. But the chance of a moment of freedom enchanted me. I had not mounted a horse since my arrival, and it had felt like a great loss. This was indeed a rare and special treat.

"I was sent to change my clothes, and a slave brought me a colorful and loose-fitting outfit — the customary outfit of the Ottoman horsemen. I hurried outside and found a stable boy waiting for me in the courtyard. He had saddled a magnificent thoroughbred for me, and I mounted with an ecstatic feeling of freedom and pride. Castriota, ready and eager on his black stallion, instructed me to keep up with his pace.

"As we set out on a frantic ride through the rolling Turkish landscape, I was certain that Castriota was trying to measure my skills as a horseman. He kept the pace for a long time, but I had no difficulty following him. It felt like it was only yesterday that I had been on horseback. It was wonderful to feel in control of such a powerful animal, and at some point I took over and put a considerable distance between me and my guide. I had no intention of escape, mind you. It was the challenge I couldn't resist.

"After a while I slowed down a bit, but I made

sure that Castriota never got the better of me. I stayed in front. Of course, it is possible that my companion willingly let me take the lead, because not once did he call me back. It seemed that he understood my need to feel completely free, if only for a little while.

"And I knew when to stop. My father had taught me well about horses, and I would never founder such a beautiful animal. I stopped in a small grove and dismounted. Castriota followed me and praised my horsemanship. He asked me to sit down with him for a while and laid out his cape for me to sit on. It was obvious that he wanted to talk to me, and I waited for him to begin.

"'You probably know that we are almost fellow countrymen,' he began. 'But you believe that I have forgotten my kin and country while spending my days in luxurious surroundings at Murad's court. You think that I am weak and indulge myself in a lazy life of abundance, completely accepting the fact that I am a prisoner.' He fell silent and leaned back, gazing thoughtfully at the sky above us. I said nothing. He had guessed my thoughts, and I had nothing to add. But I was still curious. What was on his mind? Maybe this influential man could help me gain my freedom. I found myself lost in wishful thinking as I watched him out of the corner of my eye.

"He was an older man, but his gray hair and white moustache did not conceal the fact that he was still a very strong and able-bodied warrior. He was tall and slim with a face like an oriental sage. In spite of the differences in stature and looks, there was something about the man that brought my father to mind. Maybe it was the fact that Castriota now seemed so trustworthy, or maybe it was the fact that he had acted like a parental protector by taking me away from my furious tutors. I remained cool and reserved, but in my heart I had already become his friend. These feelings surprised me. I had never thought it possible for me to change my mind about anything in such a short time. My suspicions had vanished but my common sense told me to be careful. Maybe this was just a clever plan designed to make me put my trust in Castriota.

"Castriota sighed and started to talk again. His voice was calm.

"'Murad is quite a civilized sultan. He has never underestimated the power of science and knowledge. He has never allowed religion to darken the minds of his scientists. On the contrary, from his point of view, knowledge is the path to God. Murad has a weak spot, though. He is vain and easily flattered. He sees himself as a man of the world — which of course he is, make no mistake of that — and he enjoys the company of educated Western aristocrats. In their company he is able to test the excellence of his own civilization against the famous Western culture.

"'This must be the reason that Murad very soon took an interest in me, and I jumped at the chance to gain some privileges and a secure position from where I could plan my escape. I made quite an effort to humor him and fulfill his wishes and expectations. One thing has been clear to me from the start. Never underestimate the man. He is vain, but not stupid. He will easily see through idle flattery, and if I did nothing but sit back and agree with him on every issue I would soon end up in the hole from where they took me. I kept my senses and conducted myself as his equal. In that way I could gain access to vital information. I admit that I have enjoyed debating with a man completely devoid of any Western notions. I agree with Murad that the differences between the Ottoman Empire and the Western world make an interesting debate. We have now reached a mutual understanding, and Murad has no fear of letting me out of the palace once in a while. This understanding between sultan and prisoner has brought us here today. I am the untouchable among the prisoners, and I have won a special kind of respect that only foreigners will gain at

Murad's court — the respect due to a culture considered equal to the Ottoman ways. I am still nothing but a prisoner, and Murad will never let me go. But when the time comes I will fight for my freedom and I will win.'

"Castriota paused and turned to me. Maybe he wanted to see how I was reacting so far. But I just looked back at him in silence, knowing there was more to come. I was growing even more impatient to learn why he had brought me here. Maybe he had been sent out to win my trust and then feed me false information. When released I would go straight to my father and pass it on to him. This could very well be, but my intuition told me differently. Castriota could be my friend and perhaps later a valuable ally.

"Castriota started talking again, and now he went directly to the question I wanted answered.

"'Finally I have succeeded in bringing you outside with me where no one can hear us, my young friend, Vlad Dracula. I have for some time wondered what to make of you. You seem to be a survivor. In time you will return to your country, and I feel it would be of great benefit for both of us to become allies.'

"I had not expected such a forward proposition. Nor had I expected that Castriota would actually talk about my future release as if it could become reality. I had hoped and dreamed, but I had never allowed myself to really expect anything. On the contrary, I had forced myself to expect death rather than freedom.

"Castriota seemed to sense my confusion, and he put his hand over mine, saying there was more I needed to hear. He wanted me to know what he knew, especially since this concerned my father and the situation in Wallachia.

"'Your father has been under severe pressure lately. The Christians are preparing for the final blow against the Ottoman forces. A vast number of crusaders have come to join in the battle. You know of Dracul's terrible dilemma. He can't go against his own people even if it means putting his sons' lives at stake. He has to risk Murad's revenge. Nothing has happened yet, but Murad knows that war is coming and he has no intention of letting either of you go. Radu is quite safe as Mehmed's favorite and I can personally make sure that you are not harmed either. Even so, you are probably going to endure some sort of hardship due to the way Dracul is handling the situation. I will guard your life but Murad will probably deny you any privileges from now on.

"'Please be patient and let me finish before you ask me any questions. You complained today that you have been kept in ignorance of your kin and country. Now I will try to make it up to you. Dracul has some very dangerous and powerful enemies, and the union between the Christian forces is only temporary. Right now the constant pressure from Murad's army south of the Danube has top priority, and all internal differences have been pushed aside, but only for the time being. Maybe you have heard the name Hunyadi mentioned? The White Knight of Transylvania!'

"I nodded. I was very young when I left my home, but still I remembered hearing my father talk about this man. John Hunyadi and my father had been rivals for as long as I remembered. The White Knight always seemed to be the cause of political or military difficulties in the Wallachian struggle for independence from both Ottoman and Western influences. His name was often mentioned in connection with treason and secret pacts with our neighboring countries, and stories of Hunyadi's courage and lust for power were still vivid in my mind. Apparently the Western powers had great faith in his ability to serve the Christian cause. I knew very little of his actual achievements, but the fame of the awesome White Knight of Transylvania had not escaped my attention.

"Castriota saw that I was familiar with the name, and he continued.

"'What you don't know is that your father took

Hunyadi as a prisoner a few years ago. Hunyadi had gathered what he regarded as a great army, but he needed Dracul's well-known cunning and cleverness in planning a strike against the Turks. But Dracul cast a single glance at Hunyadi's troops of 15,000 soldiers before declaring that Murad would bring twice as many on a simple hunting expedition. This offended Hunyadi terribly, and he refused to take further advice.

"'Of course the battle was lost almost as soon as it started. Hunyadi suffered utter humiliation and defeat. His men were brutally slaughtered, and he barely managed to escape without being mortally wounded himself. Dracul quickly arranged for Hunyadi's immediate arrest. A trial took place in Wallachia and Hunyadi was sentenced to jail for having led his army toward certain doom.'

"Castriota now turned to me. It was as if he wanted to look straight into my soul to find out whether or not I understood that he was going to reveal everything about my father and my home. I looked back at him, unafraid and ready to listen. After all, my life and future depended on the actions of my kin.

"'Hunyadi has already been released from prison. Your father escorted him to the Transylvanian border, and the two of them have agreed to coexist peacefully until the great battle is

fought and won. As I told you, we face very difficult times. I believe that this time the Christian
army will prove to be the strongest.

"'Murad has heard of Dracul's wholehearted
support to his Christian friends and allies, and he
will not tolerate this deceit. Furthermore, Dracul's
position is doubly risky because Hunyadi, as we
speak, is defaming his reputation by spreading lies
and evil slander. Dracul may very well be killed by
someone within his own ranks. Or his allies will
stand back and let Murad's soldiers kill him in
battle.'

"I was completely stunned by this information.
After all these years spent in complete ignorance, I
now found myself in the middle of a complicated
power struggle that might end in a devastating war
between the East and the West. Castriota's talk of
a highly strung situation within the Christian
ranks and about the critical tension between
Dracul and Murad was hardly comprehensible to
me. I had to take a deep breath in order to fathom
the consequences of a full-scale war. Would
Wallachia survive this? How would the so-called
allies act should Murad choose to cross the
Wallachian borders? Would they send soldiers to
the rescue, or would they just secure their own
border and sacrifice Dracul?

"I felt betrayed by my own father. How could

he openly let his army join the united forces against Murad? He knew the consequences of such an action. He knew what would happen to us. Murad had time and time again demonstrated his methods of retaliation. I had seen the executioners cut out the eyes of young boys because of their fathers' deceit. Why should Murad spare me?

"Now I knew that I had to assert myself in order to win Murad's respect. I could take my chances or I could lean back and wait for the executioner.

"I asked Castriota how I could win the sympathy of Murad.

"'From now on you have to stay near me. Your father is engaged in activities against Murad's interests, so your safety is at stake. For the time being Murad will wait and watch. At the first sign of movement in the Christian army, Murad will strike. Then he will decide what to do with you. You must make Murad see that you can still be of some value to him. You must remind him that you represent the future and make him think that you will always be his ally.

"'I have great interest in gaining your friendship, you know. I have been watching you for some time now. I know that you have a great future. The name Dracula will be famed and feared when your time comes. As for myself, I was born in Serbia. A group of boyars awaits my return, and they will support my claim to the Serbian throne. But in spite of this I have chosen to be patient. I have succeeded in gaining a position among Murad's trusted advisers, and I can provide information that otherwise would be impossible to get. I must stay here because Murad is working on a very ambitious and long-term project. It will take years to complete, but when that happens the world will witness the terrifying striking power of a monstrous and ingenious invention.

"'You will stay here with me. When the time is right we will both escape and return to our duties at home. Once rightfully given our birthrights it will be easy for us to join forces against the Ottoman Empire. You have the strength and cunning to rule Wallachia and I will not miss this opportunity to offer you my friendship. But, as I said, I still have reasons to stay here for some time. Escape is out of the question right now.

"'Basilica will be ready to strike in a couple of years. You have no idea of the devilish nature of this secret weapon. Basilica, a cannon 27 feet long with a 48-inch bore, will be capable of firing projectiles weighing 600 pounds, propelled by 150 pounds of gunpowder. I have heard that one single shot will leave a crater no less than six feet deep. The blast will be deafening, and the smoke will darken the sky for miles around. The cannon is a terrible weapon, created to weaken any bulwark or battlement. Just one blast is enough to kill hundreds of men.

"'I have seen the drawings myself. If everything goes as planned, the cannon will be ready before long. Murad has hired the best blacksmiths and engineers from Europe, and they are now working for a very handsome salary. Outstanding mathematicians and inventors have drawn up the designs and built several small-scale models. Every man involved has promised to deliver no less than perfection, and they have all accepted that failure will mean death. It seems that Murad is determined to get what he wants.

"'And the target for this hellraiser? Constantinople, my friend.'

"We sat in silence for a while. My mind was bursting with what I had learned. All this time in ignorance, and now suddenly I was being told what was going on around me. Castriota went on.

"'This is why the Christian army is planning to act soon. Right now they represent a significant threat to Murad's great plan. He can not engage in a war now because, if defeated, he will never be able to carry out what he calls the ultimate blow against Christianity. Murad will try to avoid any confrontation until Basilica is finished. And if Dracul can be kept from acting, there will be no confrontation between the two parties because Dracul's army is meant to spearhead the attack by the Christian forces. As you see, it is very difficult to predict what will happen. I am the very source of information they need on the other side. I am the only one who is able to send reports and warn them about Murad's most secret thoughts.'

"Castriota had now told me everything he knew. I regarded him as my friend. My reservations and fear of any hidden intentions had vanished. He had enlightened me and made my situation tolerable even though I had every reason to be disturbed by what he had told me. Castriota had given me back the sense of belonging to the Christian world on the other side of the border. He had given me the hope of getting back to my native country. Most important, he honestly believed in me and my future. For the first time I saw myself as more than just the son of Dracul. I was Dracula, the future prince of Wallachia."

LUCIA'S DIARY

June 13, 1994

Dear Grandfather,

I've been reading for hours now. It's late and my

eyes hurt but I must put down my impressions before I go to bed.

First I must tell you how much it means to me that you have shared your secret with me. You have given my life a whole new meaning by letting me into the strange and wonderful world of Dracula. It's difficult to find the words to describe how it feels to possess these old documents. When I read Maresciu's tale I also hear the voice of Dracula. Sometimes it's only a whisper and sometimes it almost blows me away.

Captain Maresciu met Dracula on his ship more than a hundred years ago. Dracula makes Maresciu listen to the story of his life in the dark Middle Ages. I am sitting here in my room in the year 1994, and I believe every word I read. I mean, not only do I believe that these documents were once written by my great-grandfather at the request of a dying man. I actually believe that what I read is the true story of a medieval prince.

I know that by saying this, I also admit that I believe in the supernatural. And so what? Dracula may be a ghost or an apparition, but what if he is more than that? What if he is the undead prince of the eastern mountains?

The tale of Maresciu reveals that it was more than just a walking corpse that made the last journey on the *Demeter*. And Dracula himself is absolutely glowing, so unlike the corpses I am used to cutting open at school. He is not dead, and I can prove that with a simple list of what death is:

1. Greenish and purple coloration of the skin. Darkens by the hour.
2. Discoloration and swelling of the face.
3. Development of blisters everywhere on the skin.
4. Bursting of blisters and shedding of the epidermis.
5. Escape of blood and other fluids from the facial orifices.
6. Presence of maggots.
7. Facial features slowly deteriorating until unrecognizable.
8. Dissolution of the body.

This is not the mark of the man who confronted Maresciu on the deck of the *Demeter*. On the contrary, it seems as if Dracula is growing younger by the minute. He goes on board as an old man, takes a very long nap and rises as a young man. When he finally reveals his true identity, he is only about thirty years old and at the height of his powers.

Wille once told me about a group of fellow researchers involved in a strange quest for the unusual and the supernatural. They were searching for fabulous monsters and mythic creatures — beings that only a few, or maybe nobody, had ever seen. Strange and ancient animals hiding in the darkness of legendary places: the Loch Ness creature and the Yeti of Tibet. Still living, extinct or never been? These scientists chose the name "crypto-zoologists" for themselves and their work. As far as I know they are still hunting for their dreams.

I remember that Wille was very impressed by their will to search for what they believed in. But he never joined them. Spiders have always been his joy and passion. He used to say that the human imagination was no match for the ingenuity of the spider and the infinite beauty of the web when a ray of sun hits the finely woven pattern of silky threads. I have never quite been able to understand this, but I do understand the passion of the crypto-zoologists.

If you negate the concept of impossibility, if you accept the notion of the universe as nothing but possibilities, your mind will expand along with the view of everything around you. Even our apparently explored and fully known world contains an endless number of ways to challenge the civilized and educated way of thinking. Freedom of the mind does not exist until the strict logic in our view of nature has been expanded to an acceptance of the illogical and the impossible. What a pity that so few people have the courage to believe in that.

I have come to share the dreams of the crypto-zoologists. I have the old documents in my possession and that is how I read them — as documentation for something that happened a long time ago. It is odd, but I am convinced that a medieval prince is actually alive today. If it is true that he stepped out on the deck to tell his tale a hundred years ago, he is still around. He can never die.

This is how I read the tale of Maresciu. This is my understanding of the strange story. Grandfather, you told me to make up my own mind about what you have given me, and so I have.

June 14, 1994

Dear Grandfather,

I have spent the whole day reading and thinking. This story is turning my world upside down, but in some odd fashion it has also cleared my mind and helped me deal with my own problems. It all comes to me as I go along with the story.

It seems so farfetched, I know. You may ask what Dracula can possibly mean to a modern person, and I find it very hard to explain myself. But there is something about the old mariner's tale. Maybe it is the voices of Dracula and his swooning prisoner on the deck. Maybe it is the papers themselves — the yellowed and crumpled sheets, the faded ink and carefully written letters. It is as if I have gotten back a vital and sadly lost part of myself. I enjoy holding the heavy bundle of papers, and I love the musty smell of them. Best of all, I can read the story any way I like, and I take my time doing so, slowly savoring each and every word.

The light is fading around me. Wille's apartment has a special charm in the dusk. The heavy curtains, the antique armchair and the bookshelves and even the wallpaper seem to shroud themselves in the warm, protecting darkness and silently greet the coming of the night. I am sitting by the window in the library. Only a single lamp is lit, an old art deco piece in the shape of a woman holding a globe of light. It is shining with a faint yellow glow, and it turns the dusk into complete blackness.

Maresciu says that Dracula, according to the legend, was the devil's apprentice. The tenth scholar of the Scholomance, the school of darkness.

The tenth pupil was to mount his dragon and assist his master. The name Dracula is derived from the Latin word, *Draco* — dragon. I remember the term because it is part of some spider's name, but I looked it up today to make sure.

But even the devil's pupil has apparently had a human life like everybody else. Dracula was born as human as any, and it is the story of this life that he forces onto Maresciu. So far, at least. But I know that Dracula is more than that. He is eternal and he is everything! Dracula is exactly what I want him to be. Or could it be that he is what Maresciu wants me to believe? Is Maresciu's voice the voice of truth?

June 15, 1994

Dear Grandfather,

In a minute I will plunge into the tale again. I will return to Murad's palace. Maybe the story will continue at a calm and steady pace, stating the simple facts of what happened during the imprisonment of the adolescent Dracula. Maybe I will be swept off my feet by the ramblings of a lunatic. No matter what direction the story will take, I will follow it.

Dracula spent his youth among the Turks. He was abruptly taken away from his home and his family. His life, from the point where I left him, is endangered by the doings of his father and the vengeful intentions of Murad. I can not help thinking of Maresciu. How did he feel when Dracula told him this part of the story? It must have thrilled him to learn about his tormenter's own story of horrors — a helpless young man at the mercy of an almighty and angry sultan. Alone in foreign surroundings, wandering among his enemies and awaiting death at any time. This must have pleased Maresciu as he lay half naked in a stupor on the cold and wet deck of the ship that was once his home and pride.

I stayed up late last night. I feel safely distanced from the world in the dark while the city is asleep all around me. I enjoy my own company and the silence of the night. Arthur has left for his summer vacation, and now I have all the time in the world to indulge myself in the documents. I actually need some time completely alone — alone with Delifrena, that is. For some time I have longed for this. I could hardly breathe around Arthur, let alone keep track of my thoughts. Now I'm free to relax, read Maresciu's tale and prepare myself for the fall term. Arthur won't be back until the end of next month, and he promised me that he would give me a call before he returns.

For the first time in my life I have actually chosen to be by myself for a while. It feels right and safe.

I have put a couple of chapters of the old papers in my briefcase. I'm going to the park where I can enjoy the sun and read. But first I must remember to feed Delifrena. I found a fly swatter in the kitchen and now I have started ruthlessly chasing prey for my hungry spider. Delifrena loves it.

Yesterday she was crawling frantically around in her glass cage, killing all the half-dead flies I had provided for her.

In the short moment that Dracula stopped and fell silent, absorbed in his own thoughts, a sudden convulsion of pain and cold stiffened my limbs. I had been lying on the deck for a long time while Dracula's voice kept my mind completely spellbound. Now that he had stopped talking, my dozing nerve fibers burst out in screaming pain. I howled like an animal. When the pain subsided a bit and left me croaking pitifully, he turned around to take a look at me. He watched me closely for a moment and then began to smile.

"You needed a reminder of your position on board my ship, Captain Maresciu. I will not have you floating off into a dreamy state where you have no idea what is reality and what is not. Now I want you to answer my questions. Who are you, and what is your mission when and if I grant you a future?"

A flaring pain was splitting my head, and my body twisted in agony. I had regained my senses, no doubt about that. I had been brutally plunged back onto the wet and cold deck of the ship, writhing in front of the green-eyed devil who just laughed at my pain. I never doubted for a moment that my life depended on his mercy. My fascination for the man vanished as the pain took hold of my body. At that moment I had only one concern. I wanted to live, and I was going to fight to keep my sanity.

I answered his mocking questions as he wanted me to.

"I am Captain Maresciu, once in charge of this ship. We are drifting and I have no control over our direction, but sooner or later we will reach the northern coast of England where we will land somewhere on the shore. My mission is simple. I will tell the story of Dracula to whoever finds me."

He was clearly satisfied. Especially by my humble squirming at his feet. The peculiar twitch around his lower lip made him look positively insane.

"Then we must continue. Never forget that my story is also the story of the lives and times of your kin, Maresciu. You are Roumanian and therefore it is your duty to pay full attention to me. Listen and learn, Maresciu!"

In a few seconds I was thrown back into my state of pleasant numbness. The pain was blown away by his unearthly magic. Still, my mind was focused and clear. Again I listened to Vlad's voice.

"Back in the palace I thought about what

Castriota had told me. I still had a lot of unanswered questions, but right now I had to consider my situation in the light of what I knew. Murad was probably soon going to retaliate. How could he sit by and watch Dracul's maneuvers against the Ottoman Empire! At any time now I expected to see a battalion of soldiers coming to escort me and my brother to the narrow courtyard where the executions and the torture took place. Castriota was the only man alive who would do anything to prevent this. My father had clearly abandoned me. Now I was forced to turn to other protectors. I was still too young and weak to take action and help myself. Besides, I trusted my new friend. Castriota had given my life new meaning. I was someone, and my time with Murad's tutors had given me important knowledge of the ways and customs of the enemy. What a waste to die now!

"Nothing unusual happened in the next couple of days. My tutors urged me to tend to my studies. Castriota often came by, and he told me he had neither seen nor heard anything indicating that Murad wanted revenge at this time. Still, he told me to prepare myself for the worst. Resistance would be futile and Castriota begged me to submit humbly if the guards came for me. And, most important, to send for him if and when that happened.

"As it turned out, Murad had no intention of letting me come to any harm. When my father made his agreement with the Sultan, he accepted the conditions of the Koran, an eye for an eye. In Murad's mind I was a substitute for Dracul's body and soul. I would be the one to pay for his mistakes. However, it was not the body Murad craved this time. On the contrary, he wanted to make sure that I adopted every single aspect of the Ottoman culture. Murad was not going to let the efforts of his best teachers go to waste by having me killed. He wanted to make me a faithful servant and future ally.

"He started by taking away most of my privileges. I did not suffer or starve, but it was enough to remind me that my life and future depended on the mercy of the Ottoman. This was Murad's first attempt to break my spirit and thus prepare me for Islamic propaganda. My daily routines were altered. At dawn, I was led from my new prison cell below ground to the small courtyard where I thought I would perish by the executioner's ax. And I was always guarded by the same two soldiers. It was impossible for me to get in touch with Castriota.

"Every day I was led to the same corner of the courtyard. There I had to stay for hours, watching the spectacle of blood, listening to the screams of pain and terror. I had never in my life witnessed such a display of methods and devices of torture. No two days were alike. There were always new things for me to learn and different scenarios to watch. Thieves, murderers and spies — they all suffered their own special punishment, and everything was handled strictly according to the letter of the Koran.

"I especially remember the stakes — sharpened and greased with the best oils available. The sentenced prisoners were led out into the courtyard and forced onto a tall scaffold. A trap door was released and the victims were thrown down at the stakes beneath. The pointed and oiled poles prevented a quick death because, in most cases, they went smoothly through the bodies without ripping the intestines. I could watch the death struggle for days. I particularly remember one victim who lingered for no less than five days.

"At this point I knew that I was not taken to the courtyard of death because Murad wanted me executed but for the simple reason that I was to watch the ghastly spectacle and praise the sultan for letting me live. Murad wanted to scare me and make me forever grateful. My rebellious behavior and self-confidence were to be broken to the point where I could be molded into a faithful servant of the Ottoman Empire. Losing the alliance with my father and Wallachia was a setback, but it could easily be replaced by my loyalty and cooperation. After all, I represented the future, being the heir of Dracul. Murad wanted my attention and my loyalty, and this was how he hoped to gain it.

"But he was wrong. I was not in the least intimidated by the horrors they unveiled for me. On the contrary, I enjoyed watching the various methods of torture. Knowing that I was quite safe from coming to the same sad end as the screaming prisoners in the courtyard, I leaned back, relaxed and concentrated fully on what was happening. I remembered every detail for later use.

"It excited me strangely to watch. I felt my face burn and my muscles tighten. I was not revolted by what I saw. It felt more like a dreamy state of forbidden pleasure. I wanted to run to the executioners and tear the blood-stained instruments from their big sweaty hands. I wanted to finish what they had started. The rush of energy made me shiver like a man possessed. But I managed to conceal my excitement. I could not afford to attract attention when I was being kept under close surveillance. Therefore I pretended to be on the verge of a breakdown, and kept praising Murad as the most glorious of sultans. I let everyone hear my prayers of gratitude and made great efforts to please my guards.

"A couple of months passed, and in addition to my daily excursions to the yard, I was kept busy reading and memorizing the Koran under the supervision of sinister priests and holy men. I made a serious effort to become acquainted with the religion and faith of the enemy. I made sure to pretend that I was on the verge of acknowledging Allah and Murad as His chosen ruler of the world. They even started to believe that I would eventually renounce the Christian faith. These fools would never know that my soul already belonged to another deity. I had been born and baptized into Christianity but I had found the way to the inseparable adversary of God. I secretly spat on the Koran and those who preached it. I already knew that I would serve the dark opposite of God for the rest of my existence.

"But in the eyes of my supervisors I was soon to be trusted completely. I never let my thoughts betray me in spite of the fact that I could think of nothing but the future and the chance for revenge. Basilica would eventually be completed and ready for battle, and by that time every road to the Christian world would be open to Murad. Constantinople, the gateway to the Western world, would suffer utter devastation if Castriota failed to get his messages across the border and warn his allies about the overwhelming power of the monstrous invention. I could think of nothing but escape.

"When I was allowed back into my former quarters I immediately called for my brother. Radu and I faced each other as complete strangers. I told him nothing of Castriota's news about Wallachia and our father as I no longer knew or trusted my own brother. He had been a child when he arrived here and his upbringing and education in Mehmed's private chambers had made him a lazy and dumb pet with no thought for anything besides his own comfort. But maybe I could get some vital information from him without arousing his suspicions. I had to know what the sultan intended to do with me now.

"Whimpering phrases of gratitude toward Murad and pretending to be petrified with fear by the mere thought of being led back to the prison below ground, I seemed to touch something unselfish in Radu. In his naive attempt to comfort me, he tried to explain the errors that had cost me months of punishment. He was completely ignorant of what went on in the world outside and could not even guess what had caused Murad's actions against me. Nor did he know that our father had almost caused our deaths by provoking the Ottoman to bloody retaliation. I let him ramble on with his infantile babble, and little by little it became possible to derive fragments of important information.

"The work with Basilica was progressing rapidly, and it was clearly expected that I no longer had any feelings of affection toward my native country. Murad expected me to be completely awed by this wonder of destruction and declare my eternal gratitude and loyalty to the superior Ottoman forces when the war started. He now regarded me as a convinced follower of the Koran.

"It was clear to me that I would achieve both trust and a great deal of freedom if I was able to keep up appearances. Radu had found that life was easy and agreeable without the troublesome bonds to a kin and country long forgotten. He needed me no more than I needed the help of my father. We were both free to pursue whatever private goals we wished.

"As expected, I regained my former privileges. My tutors were reinstated, and they treated me as if nothing had happened. This time, however, I controlled my urge to argue and rebel. Castriota came by from time to time as he used to, but he, too, was very careful in his conduct toward me. He talked to my tutors and acted as if he only attended the lessons to keep an eye on the way I behaved.

"Finally, we found an opportunity to meet without anyone seeing or hearing us. I told him that I wanted to return to Wallachia, regain my birthright and fight by my father's side. I was by now strong enough to carry the dragon's coat of arms and even assert myself as a candidate for the throne.

"Once again my friend and mentor told me to wait. For the time being it was very foolish to plan an escape. Murad was preparing for what he termed the final battle, and the palace was completely sealed off to prevent spies from taking information back and forth. The guards were on full alert day and night. It would be suicide to attempt an escape now.

"I came to my senses. Of course Castriota was right. He was a survivor, and his wise sober-mindedness had kept him alive for a long time. He had gained his position through caution and care. I trusted him fully and accepted his decision without further questions.

"But I was almost seventeen years old now, and I had no intention of spending more time than absolutely necessary in this prison. I had the strength to change the world, and every minute in Murad's palace felt like a sacrifice.

"Strangely enough, Castriota told me that Murad seemed to want me to do exactly what I had in mind — return home and take over my father's position. He regarded me vital to his plans for a future alliance with the Christian border

---

states. In his mind I would never cause any trouble by trying to serve two masters, as he believed me to have become a true friend of the Ottoman cause. I wondered about this sudden trust and my ability to gain access to my father's throne, because this would only happen if my older brother were pushed aside or killed. I had difficulties understanding Murad's certainty of my success. After all, I might be killed trying to overthrow Mircea, my older brother. Then Castriota explained to me the reason Murad felt so certain about things to come.

"The Christian army was falling apart due to internal trouble. The union of the Balkan states no longer existed. Now every kingdom sought their own goals while trying to eliminate the influence of their neighbors. Personal ambition and petty struggles had undermined the joint forces against the Ottoman enemy. Hunyadi himself had been busy plotting and conspiring against his rivals. He wanted to claim a vast portion of the Wallachian border territory. His defamation campaign against Dracul had been very successful. He was now more than willing to sell his own people to the Ottoman barbarians. He was regarded as an infidel, a traitor and Murad's spy."

June 15, 1994

Dear Grandfather,

It is evening. I long for the dusk, but it will still take hours for the sun to set. Never mind, I have found my own way of mastering night and day. The heavy crimson curtains are wonderfully efficient when drawn. They do not even allow the smallest ray of light to pass through, and they leave the room dark and sultry. The flies keep getting trapped beween the draperies, and they are quite easy to catch. The heat has made them slow and dull. I take one with every swing of the swatter; it is getting pretty disgusting with all the mushy little pieces of legs and wings of insects.

Tomorrow it will have been six months since the accident. I remembered it this afternoon, and suddenly nothing seemed right. My head began to ache and my stomach went into cramps. Just as I was starting to feel comfortable by myself the loss and grief hit me!

Arthur is far away and so is Wille. My hands are shaking and I feel like the ground is slipping away from under my feet. I'm scared, but I have no idea why. Maybe it's the loneliness. Being alone was a decision I made without consulting the demons of sorrow. My parents are gone and I will never stop mourning, but I thought that the pain would gradually fade into a dull throbbing instead of these spells of panic and depression. Today I almost fainted in the park. The world, the sunshine and the laughing children in the playground seemed abominable without my mother and father around.

I can still picture the car, Mother and Father waving good-bye as they disappeared around the corner. They always did that. I always got a little wave whenever they had to leave me for a couple of hours or so. Funny how some things never change. That's what I used to think, anyhow. I used to believe that the waving meant that time was suspended and that I would never grow up as long as they remembered to reassure me with this little ritual.

They drove off and the only thing I saw was their waving hands as they turned around the curve and disappeared. "See you soon."

I have this absurd feeling that "See you soon" is like a spell. If only I could remember the proper way to say it, it would magically make everything the way it was.

Sometimes I remember all the different things I had as a child. A rag doll, a worn and favorite pair of pants, or a drawing I had spent hours finishing. In my mind everything is still vivid and clear, though it is all long gone. I will never get back my doll with the yellow hair or my white trousers with the blue stripes. The picture I drew of our house (the smell and the taste of crayon) on coarse, grayish paper was put up on the classroom wall for a week or so. Then I brought it home with me and put it up on the wall by my parents' bed. I used odd thumbtacks — two green ones, one red and one yellow. It is all gone!

I am gone, too. I have old photos of myself as a child. In one of them I am standing in the sandpit, building castles with a little red bucket (wet sand crunching between my teeth). In another I am sitting in the swing made of old tires (burning sensation on the legs when the sun heated up the black rubber). And there is one of me crying my head off because a boy had startled me by throwing a little spider in my face. That was a long time ago, and it feels like I have faded like the snapshots. I am not sure when the face I see in the mirror now replaced my real face from back then.

I have forgotten the magic words. If only I could remember ... but how can I?

Vlad obviously never forgot his magic words. And therefore he has kept his true face.

He has kept hold of the endless space of time we all receive as children. And not only has he managed to keep it, he is also in control of it. But I must remember that he is not like us. From the day he was born, demons have been watching over him, leading him away from normality and fellow men.

My world is the world of everyone else, a place with no room for the extraordinary. Eccentric characters are pushed aside because the rest of us, the normal people, are desperately busy keeping watch over a straight and orderly society for the average citizen. Those who are different are labeled outsiders, which is pretty much the same as "loser."

Vlad told Maresciu that he, too, had to submit to the rules of his prison guards. But his spirit was never broken. He never let go of his plans for escape and revenge. He is not like people of my world. We all adapt and thereby lose the chance of ever achieving anything important in our lifetime, short as it is! I wish that I could be like him. He is the ultimate outsider, and his supernatural strong mind makes him as invulnerable and eternal as a force of nature. Maybe I can find an echo of his special gift somewhere within myself. I do not want to spend the rest of my life toiling in an unbearable race for the prize of normality.

Vlad has baffled me with his tremendous will to overcome any difficulty in order to clear the way for whatever plan he may have had in mind. Everything seems possible to him — at least he never seems to doubt this. Maybe his confidence and independence have made it possible for him to conquer time and space. His personality has never been erased or altered by the centuries. On the contrary, it is fixed in a medieval mold. In my world he would be committed as a complete lunatic.

I remember our old television set — black-and-white, of course. We had it for a long time because my father refused to buy a new one as long as the old one was still working. He never watched anything but the news, and he often told me that I ought to use my own imagination instead of watching trivial TV shows. Still, I spent a lot of time in front of the flickering black-and-white screen. Imagine, this old television set brought me my very first experience of the strange and unusual. The old horror movies (made for black-and-white television with their shimmering lights and shadows) touched me with their special kind of misery and melancholy. I remember sitting on the floor, watching and wondering why it wasn't scary. It was supposed to be terrifying. Children should be afraid to sleep alone in their beds at night after watching one of those movies, but I loved them. The sadness of Frankenstein's monster and the dreamy happiness of the vampire's victims remained a mystery. Why wasn't it scary? I watched all those old monsters in their never-ending fight for survival, and it always seemed to me that the evil came from the mob of peasants and screaming hunters with their rifles and torches. Why were the monsters pursued like that?

I asked my father and he told me to make up my own mind. He also told me that a monster would never fit in any society and therefore had to be ostracized. Of course, this didn't make any sense to me at the time, but I did see that the movies had to keep their strange world of monsters in shadows. The dark hiding places were set ablaze and the monster chased out into the brightness of the day. But by the end of each movie, I always knew that the dusk and the shadows were still lurking outside the well-lit windows. The shadow-world of the monsters would never disappear as long as the fear of darkness kept the common world in a tight grip.

As my father instructed, I made up my mind about the nature of this dark universe inhabited by monsters. It was a world of great variety. The inhabitants could be grotesque and deformed, or maybe beautiful and elegant. Their common trait was their need to stay in the shadows, out of real people's way. But the conflict between the two worlds was unavoidable. The monsters had this inexplicable urge to seek out a person from the real world, and the consequences of the meeting always turned out to be tragic. Or it could be the other way around. A misfit or a lonely person would try to explore the shadows in order to find what they sought among the supernatural beings.

The old movies depicted both worlds as lacking something vital and therefore equally forced to reach out for the unknown. No matter what, the meeting of the two different worlds was completely forbidden. Sleepwalking women, dressed in white, had to be killed by their own kind because they had crossed the limits of normality. Hunting parties set out to eliminate the alluring threat. The source of temptation had to be removed from the face of the earth. As if monsters were alien forces lurking outside the well-lit and safe houses! Bonfires were lit to cleanse the earth and prayers were said to free the community from the pollution of evil. The crowd would cheer and shout when the flames consumed another misfit.

I usually started to cry at this point. The murderous crowd hunting down every lonesome monster, the scenes of killing and destruction were ugly tableaux depicting humanity as beastly creatures running amuck. Vlad told Maresciu that he had found a dark life force in the open grave by the rampart of his father's castle in Tirgoviste. At this place he met with something unearthly, something strong enough to eliminate the rules of civilization. He felt that his most primitive and violent impulses were multiplied a thousand times in its presence.

I saw the same mechanism in the unpleasant scenes of mass hysteria. The crowd moving as one body, driven forward by hatred for the freak and a blind lust for blood.

Vlad has stepped out of the shadows (or have I let the shadows take over), and we meet whenever I take the old papers and read Maresciu's tale. I will not let him slip away. I want him to stay with me. If he is not seen by anyone else it should be safe. Maybe eventually it will be possible to erase the disturbing sound of Maresciu's voice. The old mariner has almost completed his mission and soon the story will belong to me. When I have read everything I will destroy the papers so that the story only exists through me. That is why I have to say good-bye to you, Grandfather. You will always have a place in my heart together with Mother and Father, but now I must get along on my own. I want to get away from my painful memories. It is time to change direction. But I am not leaving empty-handed. I take both the story and the belief in it. You passed it on to me, and I am forever grateful. I understand why you couldn't make up your mind about it. You left it up to me to decide.

Well, I didn't decide what to think. The powerful voice of the story decided for me. And I believe in every word he tells me.

Vlad held me spellbound by the very sound of his voice. As long as he spoke I knew that I would be shielded from the cold and the pain. I only feared the end of his story, the end of our journey. When he no longer found it worthwhile to keep me lingering in No Man's Land, I would have to return to reality, and die. There would not be much time left. I wondered who would find me on this wreck of a ship, carry me ashore and listen to the strange tale I had promised to tell. Who was all this meant for?

Vlad was inside my mind, keeping me alive by lending me some of his own life force. But every word he spoke drained what little strength I had left of my own. He was sucking my life away and replacing it with his own — ordering me to renew the memory of his unearthly existence by passing it on to the people in the Western part of the world. He was prolonging and strengthening his own life by using me.

I looked up as he began to speak. He obviously enjoyed talking about the past, and suddenly he reminded me of a tribal storyteller, seated by the fire with eager listeners gathered around him. Only here the red, hot flames were replaced by blue, cold lightning flickering around us.

"Cazan brought me the news of my father's death. He came to me in the beginning of 1448, the last loyal boyar from my father's dissolved council. He had succeeded in finding his way to Adrianople. He arrived wounded and exhausted on the back of a half-dead hack barely able to carry him to the gates of the city. He was greeted by Murad who, on learning that Dracul was dead, immediately sent for me. I was officially declared a free man as Murad told me that he had nothing to gain by keeping me hostage any longer."

Vlad was kneeling down beside me. He put both his hands on my face, and I felt as if I had drawn my last breath. I was suffocating from the rotting stench that filled my nostrils, and the deck seemed to disappear beneath me. I threw my head back in a desperate movement and gasped for air. Everything went completely dark around me. I took another deep breath ... and found that my body was gone. I was floating in the air, still in possession of all my senses. I heard and saw everything more loudly and clearly than ever before, without any bodily limitations.

I saw that I was in Murad's throne room.

Shining fabrics and glowing colors mixed with the flickering light from hundreds of oil lamps. The silky draperies were woven in fine patterns so full of exquisite details that I found an abundance of beauty in every little piece of embroidery.

Three men are present in the room. Murad, imposing and austere, leans back on the costly cushions. His long, carefully combed and oiled beard flows down the crimson caftan. His big turban resembles a giant, golden onion growing out of his forehead. He is silently watching the reaction of the young Vlad while the old tattered warrior, Cazan, recounts the events leading to the fall of Dracul. They both seem absorbed in the conversation, though Murad is closely observing their shifting facial expressions. Cazan is kneeling in front of the young Dracula while bringing the sad news of the death of both Dracul and Mircea. Vlad is standing motionless, still very young and thin with a narrow and sullen face. But his eyes are the same as ever — piercing and glowing from within. He is dressed in the oriental manner with the loose, flowing garments hanging from his body as if there is nothing beneath.

I listen to the low voice of Cazan. Apparently he had been with Dracul at the time of Tirgoviste's downfall. The frenzied citizens had gathered in the streets, cursing Dracul for his dealings with the

Ottoman Empire. It had not been possible to stop the tidal wave of hatred and frustration. Hunyadi and his allies had succeeded in starting a civil war. The campaign against Dracul had turned out as he had hoped. No one dared defend Dracul at this point. Anyone who didn't follow the crowd was struck down and killed.

Dracul and Mircea were trapped in the castle. The furious masses had forced their way into the courtyard with torches and drawn swords. However, Dracul had no intention of escape. He ordered the few loyal soldiers he had left to fight by his side. They stepped outside and faced the crowd, determined to die fighting. Which, of course, they did very quickly. Mircea was surrounded and overpowered in less than a minute. They dragged him to the northern rampart, whipped him unconscious and buried him alive among the murderers, deserters and spies. Dracul managed to escape while everybody attended the gruesome execution of his son. Followed by a couple of his boyars he reached the village of Balteni before they were ambushed by a group of hired assassins. Dracul was mercilessly cut down and left lying on the moor outside the village. They were all killed except Cazan. He was wounded in the head and lay motionless in a pool of his own blood. The gang of killers assumed that he was dead like the rest. When he regained consciousness there was nothing to do but call to some friendly peasants to bury the dead.

Dracul wasn't buried with the boyars. Cazan had him taken to the nearby Chapel of Snagov. Dracul had had it built a few years earlier. The chapel was located on a little island in Lake Snagov. It had walls as thick as any fortress, and this special place had been carefully chosen because of its natural protection against enemies. Dracul was buried there.

Vlad said nothing and didn't move a muscle until Cazan had finished. His face was pale and he looked almost insignificant standing beside the old rugged warrior and the imposing figure of the sultan. I was aware that this moment was important and that the young Vlad had now reached a turning point. He had brought me here to watch this special hour of transformation.

The young prisoner lifted his head and started to change before my eyes. He had listened to Cazan without making a sound or lifting an eyebrow, but now his idle dreams of revenge and glory suddenly turned into reality. The time for action had finally come.

On his face there was no trace of sadness over the loss of his father as he became aware that now he was next in line for the throne of Wallachia. He had to win it back and defeat Hunyadi once and for all. I saw the relentless killer come to life, and there was no doubt in my mind that Dracula would serve only his own purposes from this moment on.

June 16, 1994

Vlad,

You chose Maresciu and made him serve as your link to the Western world. You allowed him to see straight into your world.

Only my family knows about your journey, and I am the only reader alive. Did you foresee that I would eventually be the one to read your story and understand it? Do you know what I am going to do now?

I will allow you to come closer. I am inviting you in. You couldn't get aboard the ship without Maresciu's consent. Without an invitation you cannot enter. This much I know!

Delifrena is breeding.

I take care of her and make sure that she has everything she needs. Her little crawling offspring are already taking an interest in the flies that I provide for them. All this is happening because I have made it possible. Delifrena is breeding because she senses that it is time to welcome new life. And now

I say, "Welcome, enter freely and of your own will. Let me share the happiness you bring. Let me share your world!"

MARESCIU'S TALE

I was floating weightless and invisible in Murad's throne room. I had witnessed Cazan bringing the message of death to the young Dracula and I had heard Murad declare his period of imprisonment terminated. I watched everything with exhausting eagerness. It felt as if someone was sucking every last spark of life out of me, but I still couldn't tear myself away from the spectacle.

Cazan solemnly handed the young Vlad two objects. The inheritance from father to son — obligation and inspiration. The heavy Toledo sword and the golden buckle from the coronation ceremony in Nuremberg. My vision was gradually blurring as I was pulled back to the *Demeter*'s icy deck, but before I completely lost my bearings I witnessed the total transformation of Vlad. He put down his father's belongings for a moment while taking off the long, hampering robe. Then he hung the sword around his waist and fastened the buckle. While holding the sword tightly, he swore that Hunyadi would pay for what he had done. He seemed to look straight at me (though I was invisible — floating silently above him without my body) as if to assure me that this was not just idle talk. He suddenly looked taller, and his eyes burned into mine as I was slowly swept backwards, out of the room and away.

White light flooded the room, but the sight of Vlad bracing himself for the future battle against his rivals for the Wallachian throne was imprinted on my memory. My eyes were blinded by the light but I still heard the same hoarse voice I had listened to in the fog and rain aboard the ship. With Cazan and Murad as witnesses he made the solemn promise that he was going to win back his father's throne and slay every last one of Hunyadi's men. I couldn't see him anymore, but I felt the hate and eerie exhilaration in his eyes when he said that.

The flaring white light exploded in my brain when I woke up on the slimy boards of the ship. The pain of body and soul was excruciating, but at least it assured me that I wasn't dead yet. I looked up and met the staring eyes of the creature I had just left in Murad's palace. He had lived for centuries and still the vivid glare of eternal youth was unaltered. It made me squirm fearfully beneath the towering figure. I could hardly separate the two Draculas — the youth in Murad's palace and the loathsome creature standing before me on my ship — and I could tell by the look on his face that all along he had hoped for the killing of his father and brother. He had patiently waited for the moment when he would have the chance to take over. He didn't want revenge as much as he wanted unlimited power. Now the time had come for him to take on the role of the tyrant. The Draculs still had loyal supporters in Wallachia, and he just had to wait for the opportunity to claim back the throne.

We were both silent. I was painfully aware of every limb in my body and I knew that the monster would let me feel how exhaustion and deadly cold would eat their way into my bones. He continually tried to steal my mental faculties. He hadn't succeeded yet, but soon my resistance would succumb to his destructive powers. I was becoming rapidly weaker and I felt his determination to eliminate what was left of my will power. I no longer thought that I could survive this journey. He had never regarded me as a fellow Roumanian, an ally taking on the mission of recounting the tale of the famous Dracula. He was gradually destroying my mind in the effort to make me his sleepwalking slave with only one assignment before the final destruction. He didn't want my mind and my voice to distort his tale in any way. I had to die, and still carry out his wishes.

He silently let the cold stiffen my limbs.

June 16, 1994

I feel sleepy and I'm shivering with cold. The chill must be imaginary because right now we are experiencing the hottest summer in years. A strange lethargy makes my limbs heavy and numb. Yet it feels as if I am floating on icy waves. The flies are buzzing in the window. They are big and fat. Some are sitting completely still in the draperies. I have sealed off everything. Every fly in this room will certainly be dead by tomorrow. Delifrena will have a feast.

I am floating peacefully and thoughtlessly. Maresciu is changing. His voice is fading. Is the story rewriting itself, or is it me? Am I the one who is changing? I wanted Maresciu out of the way. And now he is fading!

But I will not read anymore tonight. I could easily pick up the papers and exhaust him until his voice is completely gone. But if I just lean back and wait one more night, it may save me the trouble. He is already transparent and weak.

Delifrena is looking at me, her eyes glowing in a manner I have never seen before. Green eyes, shining dully through the dimness of the room.

Her offspring are crawling around her.

Vlad,

I have read Maresciu's tale — your tale. It is time for me to take over. I will do my own writing from now on. That is, I will rewrite every single word said by Maresciu. I must take my part in this spectacle of sound and fury.

But let Maresciu have his last say!

He is still speaking to me. The whispering voice has taken on a strange, monotonous rhythm. It makes me drowsy ... the words are echoing in my ears. Drowsy ... my vision is blurring ... he is talking to ... not to me any longer ...

Who is she ... where ... when?

"All good things come to those who wait. Dracul and Mircea were dead, but it was not yet time for me to settle on the Wallachian throne.

"By the end of 1448 Castriota had returned to his native country and there he was awaiting the advancement of John Hunyadi's mercenaries. We both knew that Hunyadi was going to move in on Serbian territory in order to carry out his ambitious plan — create a wall of his own soldiers to prevent the Ottoman army from gaining access to any Balkan kingdom, thus earning him the right to dominate the Eastern European world.

"As we expected, Hunyadi came ...

"Castriota met him outside Kosovo. They fought, and Castriota defeated his army to the last soldier. Only Hunyadi was taken alive. This was done on my request and Castriota kindly obliged me. Hunyadi was put in chains and taken to the blackest pit in Castriota's fortress.

"I traveled to Kosovo. By leaving the Wallachian court I knew that usurpers would do whatever they could to prevent my return, but it didn't matter. At the time revenge was infinitely more important than the Wallachian throne. I would have the opportunity to reclaim my birthright. Hunyadi, however, couldn't wait."

Maresciu is dead. There is no other explanation. Besides, I can feel it. I see shadows flowing behind the words, exactly the way Maresciu himself sensed and suffered Dracula's tale.

I begin reading the prosaic, monotonous narrative. Vlad speaks in a peculiar chanting voice, as if he is telling the tale of some strange, ancient hero. I am reading but my concentration is slipping. I stare desperately at the pages, increasingly dizzy by the second. The words take control of my mind ... I must follow the sound of his voice.

A bright, white light suddenly stuns me. Slowly the light fades and my vision clears. I can see shapes and movement. At first they seem dim and dreamlike. Then my focus sharpens and I understand. Vlad has brought me with him back to the life that was once his. Maresciu is no longer here. I am.

Horsemen are coming. Vlad on his swift horse followed by soldiers. They only stop to get fresh horses. I see the sun setting and the moon rising. Again and again — only a few minutes between night and day.

Now I see a fortress on the horizon. A river in front of it. Vlad is speeding his horse on. The bleak fortress belongs to Castriota.

The two men are standing face to face in the courtyard. They embrace. Castriota, tall, sinewy and venerable. Dracula, of lesser height but muscular build (for the first time I really see him!). His long auburn hair tied in a leather string. He is grimed with dust and sweat but his eyes reveal no fatigue. I recognize those eyes — from where I do not know.

They enter through a large iron-plated door. I am strangely nauseated but I follow them inside. It's like looking through a long black tunnel. Castriota and Dracula are small figures ahead.

I know where they are going. To the dungeons. Now they are descending — calmly down to hell, it seems. The darkness is damp and a moldy smell overwhelms me. There is something else. An odor I cannot place or describe.

They stop by a narrow door. It rumbles and shrieks as they open it. A terrible stench is flushed against us. I feel so sick. We are in the dungeon.

It is filthy beyond belief. I only see vague shadows by the light of Castriota's candle. The darkness must be hellish black when the door is shut. We are in some sort of narrow passage, keeping close to the slippery stone wall as we pass a row of animal cages. I can find no other words for them. The floor is covered with rotten straw and we hear the hoarse, beastlike moaning of the hunched figures behind the bars.

We reach the other side of the horrible crypt and yet another door is flung open. The sallow gleam of the candle reveals a horrifying pit. No iron bars are needed in here. The clammy, rotten dampness is incomparable. The candle almost suffocates from lack of oxygen. The floor is covered with some hideous substance, almost knee deep. Dear God, it is human feces! A figure lies sprawled by the wall.

Hunyadi!

I can hardly see him. Vlad takes the candle and stands contemplating for a long while. I am floating and suddenly I find myself in front of him. He is smiling — a strange, twitching grimace — and again he turns to Castriota.

I feel myself drawn backwards. The last thing I perceive down below is the sound of a summoned guard. Suddenly I understand every word of this foreign language.

I am back in the courtyard. The clean, fresh air feels like a blessing. I will never forget the dungeon's horror. Vlad and Castriota are returning, too. A table and chairs are brought out. They seem to be preparing a feast. The plates and cups are heavy and priceless. The tablecloth is made of fine crimson material. The food is served by silent, humble women.

The two men take their seats. They start eating.

Now a platoon of armed soldiers marches into the courtyard. A few minutes later more soldiers follow. They carry only some long, finely pointed wooden poles ... or lances. The soldiers take their places by the table where Vlad and Castriota are finishing their meal, seemingly unconcerned by anything. A strange stillness haunts the place.

Then they come. A stunned, soiled figure is dragged out into the open. Almost bereft of any human likeness, Hunyadi makes feeble, crawling movements on the stony yard. A gigantic guard kicks him toward the table.

I feel a panging headache explode behind my eyes. What torture to watch the gruesome spectacle evolve in front of me.

Vlad is calmly wiping his mouth with a silk napkin. He stands up and walks slowly around the table. Hunyadi, or what's left of him, croaks some inarticulate sounds. He can hardly move.

Vlad claps his hands and eyes the prisoner, a piece of human flesh barely alive, lying by his feet. It is his moment. He has been waiting patiently for this. He is in no hurry. Castriota is leaning back in his chair, his face completely expressionless.

Then it happens! Vlad virtually explodes in a roaring outburst. He lifts the pointed pole and thrusts it right through Hunyadi's unprotected belly. Everything is white, glaring pain. I can not escape but my focus is mercifully blurred. Still, I see the terrible stabs. One by one, with long pauses in between. The impaled victim is writhing pitifully ... awfully. I hear the wheezy sounds coming from his throat.

Finally Dracula, the Impaler, ends the suffering of the bleeding man. He raises the lance for the last time. Now it is pointed directly at Hunyadi's heart. He thrusts it down, and I am slowly dragged backwards into a thick, white fog.

It is dawn. I must have slept right here in my chair. I have been sick all over myself. There is vomit on my blouse. I need to take a bath, but I have to write. I must finish what I have started. I must keep on writing no matter what.

The piercing rays of the sun hurt my eyes. It feels as if little needles are cutting through my skull. I am sick again. Cramps and convulsions.

What is happening?

I wrote something last night. I don't remember what.

Vlad,

I have gone too far, too fast! But I will keep rewriting Maresciu's tale because I have seen you. My eyes are still burning from the scorching light. Well, it is done. I have let you into my world and you have let me into yours. But who is in control? What happens next?

I am searching for the voice of Maresciu. I turn the pages of the old document and still I see my great-grandfather's handwriting. I must admit I sort of expected to see the ink erased, but the handwriting is still there, clearly visible underneath my own scribbling.

I will not go out today. I have to regain my strength and continue what I have started.

If Maresciu is still around, I must finish reading his story. If he is gone I will have to finish writing it myself. The tale must be completed. In the end we will see whose voice will be heard.

He is still holding me back. I can feel the heavy pressure of his cold and clammy hand on my shoulder. I try to turn my aching head and notice his fingers. I haven't really given it any thought until now, but I see that they are extremely hairy with long and sharply cut fingernails. I especially notice the nails because they are clawing my thick coat, cutting right through the heavy fabric and digging deeply into my flesh.

I am not dead yet. I wish I was.

The familiar dizziness overwhelms me. I know what it means. I am going on yet another hellish journey. This will almost certainly drain what is left of my strength.

The white light. Colors and shapes appear and I see ... a traveling party ... horsemen. Vlad is leading them on as they rush forward at an unbelievable speed. The sound of the galloping horses is thundering in my head. The white light is blurring my vision. I can hardly see, until a large dark shadow appears. It is a castle, a fortress.

They cross over a drawbridge. The rumbling and shouting are echoing in my skull.

In the courtyard a tall, imposing man steps forward to greet the travelers. Vlad dismounts and returns the host's hearty embrace. They stand like that for a while, like lovers.

I still feel his hand on my shoulder. He is squeezing the air out of me. I can't breathe anymore.

The two men are standing frozen in front of me. They are as still as a grotesque statue, while I am tortured by the hard and ever-tightening grip of his hand.

Something snaps inside of me. A quick, brittle sound followed by a blissful sense of freedom. The iron grip is loosening, my body is no longer my prison. I see terrible scenes in the courtyard, but now as an unmoved spectator. Abuse, torture, blood and killing. I don't care. Vlad has let me go. I can feel another soul taking my place as a witness to the monster's unspeakable crimes. I sense someone else's fear growing in the space around me. I'm fading ... slowly dying. The two figures are still standing in a silent embrace. Only ... it's no longer two men! Vlad is holding a woman. His long hair covers her face and his cape is drawn tightly around her. I only see her as a slight shape beneath the coarse material.

In front of them lies a mangled body with a long stake driven through the heart. Vlad's victim! An ecstatic bloodfever is tinting the whole atmosphere around the couple.

I am free. Someone else has taken my place — forever!

June 18, 1994

I must have slept again. I stayed in my chair by the window to finish my reading of Maresciu's tale. I must have fallen asleep. I still feel sick. I woke up all tangled up in the long, heavy curtains. There is an odd smell about the fabric. I can't quite place it.

I'm sick.

June 19, 1994

Vlad,

My sense of reality is slipping. Am I with you? Are you with me? Right beside me in these rooms?

This I know for sure. Maresciu is no longer with us. I have spent twenty-four hours reading, and I know what is happening. The writing, the tale, is forcing me on. Maresciu's last words overlap mine. We were both there, in the exact same place. We saw the same scenes.

I must have written it down in some weird trancelike state. I don't remember doing so, but each letter is written by me. I do remember being on a journey to a strange, ancient place — another world, perhaps even another dimension.

We met. In a universe foreign to both of us — a new world for us to conquer. Our world.

I will be ready for our next encounter. Now the tale is coming to life. I don't know why I keep referring to it like that. It is not some ancient mariner's tale. I am living it as a dream, no, as a reality brought forth from the old documents. "It" has released itself from my mind and has grown strong enough to enclose me, body and soul.

I have been preparing myself in front of the mirror. My face was looking drawn and lifeless from these late-night exertions. It took little, however, to change it. Some black kohl, some lipstick — "Flaming Red" — and face powder — "Alabaster."

I am ready for you.

The following part of the tale is written in Lucia's handwriting. It is only partly distorted by a certain old-fashioned gothic quality and I am therefore absolutely certain that my niece wrote this, thinking that Vlad was speaking to her and putting down every word of his strange confession. What puzzles me is the fact that the paper it is written on is exactly the same yellowed and old material as the other pages. How this can be I can only guess.

Wilhelm Mørck

WORDS FOR LUCIA

Welcome aboard, Lucia. You have finally taken your place beside me on the slippery deck of the

Demeter. You seem transparent and ghostlike, but before long you will take on stronger colors. Be patient and savor every word I say.

I waited eight years for the moment of the final pursuit to arrive. Wallachia and all of Eastern Europe had suffered a period of great turmoil and confusion, and alliances were crumbling. Sultan Murad died in 1451. He fell from his horse for no obvious reason — as if he had been slain by the hand of Allah. He was forty-seven years old and had never displayed any signs of weakness.

Murad's son, Mehmed, immediately took up an entirely different strategy against the Western world. He was dangerously ambitious and absolutely ruthless, and much too preoccupied with all sorts of bizarre excesses for his own good. I therefore had no choice but to cancel my alliance with the Ottoman Empire.

I left Adrianople for Transylvania where my father's faithful boyars had secured enough votes for me to be elected military governor. Without Hunyadi, there was no other man suited for the post.

Basilica, the wonder of destruction, was ready for battle. The Ottoman engineers had by now learned to handle both gunpowder and other explosives and they wouldn't hesitate to make full use of them. There was no doubt in my mind that

Constantinople was Mehmed's first target. He was going to use Basilica to crush the city walls, causing devastation and death on a scale previously unheard of.

Of course I had to do whatever it would take to prevent this from happening. I possessed important information about the Ottoman military. I also knew a great deal about the year-long process of planning the attack. Castriota had generously shared every piece of information with me. Now I was ready to join with every European force in what I believed to be the final battle between two irreconcilable worlds.

Safely back in Transylvania, at the ceremony of my appointment as military governor, I renewed my father's oath of allegiance toward the Dragon Order. A set of capes, one green and one black, were quickly made for me along with a standard of the Dragon.

My pledge was not given a moment too soon. Mehmed had almost surrounded Constantinople, and it grew steadily more impossible for the Byzantine forces to meet the threat outside the city walls. Without reinforcement from the Western allies, Constantinople simply couldn't muster enough soldiers to cover the fourteen miles of walls and towers built around the city. In the light of the huge size of the Turkish army, the terrible commitment of Sultan Mehmed and the extremely weak position of the beleaguered city, the Christian leaders started to withdraw from their promise to protect the frontiers from the Ottoman threat.

I had hoped to muster a significant army and march against the Ottoman forces by land, but now it was too late. No military aid reached the battleground in time.

On May 25 the Ottoman guns released a thunderous fire against the city walls. The powerful Basilica was only fired a couple of times, but the destruction was devastating. I was still in Transylvania when the message was brought to me. "May 28, 1453. Constantinople has fallen." Mehmed II was proclaimed the victorious ruler of Constantinople, the Ottoman sultan who succeeded in making the Ottoman Empire a part of Europe. He had achieved what he wanted. His dream of fame had come true and he henceforth became known as Mehmed Fatih, meaning Mehmed the Conqueror. The Turks had gained what they had wanted for centuries. Reaching the European continent, they had taken a position from which nothing could drive them back.

In Rome the loss of Christian blood was lamented, but no one spoke of the secret shame that the Holy Roman Church had failed miserably to support the outmost bastion of the Christian world. The hypocrisy prevailed.

I witnessed this pitiful opportunism and became aware that Christianity, or rather the Roman preaching of Christianity, had its serious flaws. I could no longer take the same path as the miserable priests and bishops of the Roman Church and therefore chose to renounce my former leaders.

LUCIA'S DIARY

June 21, 1994

Vlad,

You continue your narrative of breathtaking events as if nothing has changed. Historical battles relived, wars and political games totally excluding the world of women. You have allowed me to see behind the veil of my reality, but still I am not entirely a part of yours.

Constantinople was destroyed, and neither you nor the rest of the Christian world tried to prevent it. But you never joined the hypocritical denials of responsibility. That saved you. The fall of Constantinople was the fall of the Christian frontier, and that made you strengthen your own spiritual integrity. You haven't let anybody into that special world of yours, but I know that it has room for me, too. It is a space without the limitations of nature and civilization, and yet I know that you live by some mysterious code of your own.

Delifrena has devoured her offspring. I feed her all the flies I can possibly catch but still it is not enough. She is insatiable, and I can't keep up with her hunger. I sleep in the daytime now. It is impossible for me to endure the heat and glaring light of the sun. It makes me feel faint and numb. Since I stopped going to the park during the day, the oppressive sadness has vanished and I feel more vigorous than ever. I feel so alive at night, sitting in the soft darkness with only the little art deco lamp lit so that I can read. The lamp only provides a small circle of light and the rest of the apartment is completely dark. Still I move around as I please because now I can actually sense everything around me and therefore easily find my way into any corridor of this place.

You seem so distant. I hear your voice speaking to me through the writing but I only feel your presence in short, sensational flashes. I know that I have to be patient. You haven't finished your story. But there is not much time. Arthur has written that he is returning home early. He expects to be in Copenhagen in a few days. I don't know what to do. I don't want him here but I can't get in touch with him before he arrives. It is very inconvenient that this should happen right now, because he wants to live here with me until he can get a place of his own. He gave notice on his rented rooms before he left because he had planned to travel for quite some time. As it turns out, he can't stand traveling alone. He seems to think that he can stay here with me for several weeks.

I don't want him to return, but how can I explain this in a way that he can possibly understand? I don't fully understand what is happening myself but I do know that I resent company of any kind right now. Any human kind, that is!

We have to go on. We will not be bothered for at least a couple of days. Where did I leave you ...

WORDS FOR LUCIA

In my headquarters in Sibiu, Transylvania, plans to fight my way back to power in Wallachia were taking form. Since Hunyadi's death, his army had kept the country in a state of havoc and confusion. Peasants and noblemen fought each other and made up their own laws as they went along. My father's kingdom was disintegrating in violence and crime. Gangs of thieves and highwaymen roamed about, and every citizen in Wallachia soon learned to fight for himself in order to survive.

Meanwhile, I was still waiting for something to signal my successful return to the Wallachian throne. My army was prepared to set out at short notice. We were all impatiently waiting for the sign! In Tirgoviste a large number of my father's loyal supporters were waiting for news of my return.

Finally the signal was given. The sign, foretold a long time ago by Murad's fortune tellers, appeared on the sky in the sixth month of the year 1456 and stayed there for seven weeks and four days. During this time the night sky was lit up by a glowing star with no less than six tails of fire. Murad's fortune tellers had been right! As I raised my eyes and gazed at the wonderful phenomenon, I knew that from now on nothing could stop me. It was time to depart for Wallachia!

For years I had been preparing for this home-coming. Now hundreds of boyars were awaiting my army. They were on a constant lookout for the dragon banner and whenever it appeared on the horizon a riot would begin within the walls of Tirgoviste. My father's city was certainly not going to present any resistance of importance.

We reached our destination before the end of June. The defending army of Wallachia's puppet regime had already taken position on the plain right outside the city walls. At first it appeared that we were facing an army of equal strength, but then my men caught sight of the beautiful towers of

Tirgoviste. The desire to triumphantly march through the streets to the old fortress of Dracul where the image of the dragon and the Wallachian eagle once again would appear on the parapet seemed to make them certain of their victory.

I ordered my troops forward and, as expected, our adversaries soon lost pace. By sundown exhaustion started to weaken them. My men, on the other hand, never felt any fatigue despite the fact that they had been on the march for weeks. They ignored their wounds and kept gaining ground. The last rays of the sun were redder than blood and seemed to reflect the roaring force of my fighting men. I was riding ahead of the lancers alongside the enemy's flank. The thundering sound of the horses' hooves filled my ears. Everything was tainted red by the setting sun, and as I impaled a Hungarian knight on my lance I felt myself thrown back in time.

Years ago, when I had been standing in the criminal's grave, I had only vaguely sensed the potential of this place. Now that I was only a short mile from the castle, I understood the importance of my return. The force of my childhood revelation rushed through me, and now I knew that it was coming from my own body. It came from somewhere within me, and it had always been the counterpart to my Christian roots. It was what made me superior to my fellow men, and I felt certain that from now on nothing could go wrong. I was bound to reach further than any other dragon knight because from this moment I knew the nature of my power and I would never hesitate to use it.

The wriggling body on my lance felt weightless as I flung it to the ground and watched the last glow of the red sun disappear on the horizon. My men forced themselves onward, cutting the enemy down as if they were fighting scarecrows. Now the darkness settled around us and the glowing celestial body appeared as an immense shooting star. The last defenders of Tirgoviste laid down their weapons and so, at last, we went unhindered through the gates of the city.

LUCIA'S DIARY

June 22, 1994

Vlad,

I woke up in time to see the sun set above the many church towers of Copenhagen. It was redder than I ever remember seeing it. The Round Tower, Christian IV's old observatory, looked massive and plump as the red glow from the evening sun hit its walls. Looking at it, I suddenly had an idea. I went through the books in Wille's library and found exactly what I was searching for. Now I know the celestial body that appeared in the sky for so many weeks, foretelling your victory on the plain of Tirgoviste. It was finally named two hundred years after that glorious day in 1456. You were guided to Tirgoviste by Halley's comet with its six tails of fire! Do you know that it's a regularly appearing phenomenon? It's very difficult to predict its cycle, but I actually saw your lucky star only eight years ago. This brings us even closer to each other. I have seen what you have seen. Finally I have something other than just these old papers. We live in the same world. The comet has appeared before both of us.

WORDS FOR LUCIA

She who welcomes me must welcome my world as well. I will live forever, but only if I can keep my enemies out of the dark corridors that protect me from exposure and disintegration. I only appear to those who dare to meet me where I live, without the oppressing fear of death. Death's nature is annihilation and I have conquered that. The vile essence of life is final disintegration in the black soil of the earth.

I made my choice a long time ago. I turned my back on life and gained an eternal existence outside the bright reality of mankind. I gain my strength from the soil in which I sleep. The earth will never take hold of my body. It offers protection from everything that threatens my existence, but only as long as my sleep is not disturbed by intruders. That is why I never let anybody near me. That is why I can only live in people's dreams, far away from the world that is hostile to mine. If you dare follow me, you must change as I have done. And remember that the choice you make is irretrievable.

June 23, 1994

Vlad, my love,

I will follow you if you let me. Still you haven't allowed me to see your whole world and I know that you expect me to do something. Maybe you want some act of renouncement, something to assure you that I am going wholeheartedly into your eternal night. Let me tell you that I am not just sitting here in passive longing for someone to pick me up and take me away. I am coming to meet you halfway between my world and yours. You see, I hate the ways of the nineties — the petty struggling and striving for wealth in a civilization of nothing but clerks. I want a life without any kind of compromise, and when I make a choice it is always final. I will gladly trade my world for yours, even if it means burning every bridge behind me. In fact, I have already done that. I am going to push aside anything that can possibly prevent me from doing what I want. I also know the exact point of transition. You chose the *Demeter* a hundred years ago. This is where I will meet you when the time comes to leave the world I know.

WORDS FOR LUCIA

The coronation ceremony took place in the heat of the great victory. I took my seat on the Wallachian throne but there was still much work for me to do. Wallachia had become a wilderness of crime and hypocrisy, and I had to prepare a thorough purge.

Three days of celebration passed. The old boyars of Tirgoviste gave their solemn promise of loyalty to their new ruler. Most of these men were Hunyadi's former puppets, and I knew that their promises were never to be trusted. Some of them were even busy plotting against me while they pretended to approve of my return.

When the festivities finally came to an end, everybody awaited my first action as ruler. They didn't have to wait long. The boyars personally involved in the plot against me were eliminated immediately. I summoned them along with their families, and I had the stakes raised in the courtyard. I made them line up for the execution. No one could be spared. It would be too risky to let anyone from these hostile families live. In time they might return to avenge their fathers and brothers. So, of course, I had them all pierced at the stakes — women, children, old and young.

Having disposed of these gross traitors I turned to the problems of my country in general. My father's castle in Tirgoviste was in bad shape. I needed better quarters. After some thought I found a way to combine revenge and useful slavery.

All those who had known about the plot against me, without reacting or reporting it, were invited to celebrate Easter at my castle. I prepared for the arrival of my many guests by decorating the halls and laying out soft carpets everywhere. When all the candles were lit and everything looked brilliant and festive, I took my place by the door to welcome everyone. They all came in their very best attire, expectant and thrilled to be invited. I don't recall any of them taking heed of the proper cause for the celebration — the crucifixion, the death and rise of Christ.

Having welcomed everyone, I led them to the table and offered them the best meal possible. I wanted everything to be perfect. They sat gorging for hours, never suspecting anything until I interrupted the feast and sent the musicians away. My soldiers took their positions in front of the doors. Everyone had stopped eating and silence prevailed. It was a tense but contented silence. They obviously thought that I was going to make a pleasant speech. I told them to rise from the table and prepare to march to the old ruin of a fortress outside town. This was the building site of my new headquarters and my esteemed guests were the free labor, hired for life.

At first they didn't seem to understand. Everyone started to laugh but stopped as my soldiers began to push them through the door leading outside to a dirt road that would take them to my father's castle. It was in deplorable condition. It had been robbed of every valuable item and it lacked every improvement necessary to make it a royal residence.

The ruin was situated a mile or so outside the city walls. It was well placed on a precipice by the river Arges. It had once been a splendid edifice, constructed by the master builders of the past. Now I wanted it rebuilt and restored. That was the reason I didn't kill the noble families connected with the traitors of my court. I found there was some poetic justice in letting these people slave for the construction of a new fortress for their master. It was time for them to prove the sincerity of their pledge of undivided loyalty toward their prince.

Of course, I wasn't completely unreasonable. The very old and the disabled were led down to the kitchen, where they would be given menial tasks. Only the healthy and strong were taken to the site of the ruin. Their future consisted of offering their strength to rebuild each old watchtower and piece of wall. They were going to work to their last breath.

And so off they went. It was a regular Easter parade with all the fine dresses and glittering jewels. My soldiers led them on and as I watched, it seemed that there was only a band missing — and happy faces! Everyone had become deadly pale as the seriousness of the situation dawned on them.

Thus I initiated my reign as absolute monarch.

LUCIA'S DIARY

June 25, 1994

Vlad, my love,

I am sleeping again. I feel languid and whenever I wake up I only want to go back to sleep. It feels like I am living in a dream, though I have a painfully acute perception of what is going on around me.

Delifrena is insatiable. The flies no longer suffice. I have chosen to let her out of her cage so that she can find her food elsewhere. She is free but still she stays very close to me. This evening I noticed two little red dots on my neck. I know what they are. It feels like a rash but otherwise there is no noticeable reaction. Maybe the langour? Anyway, I know that the change has started. I can't wait for it to happen. I trust that we shall meet in a short time.

June 27, 1994

Arthur has called. He is coming tonight. I am not worried about him any longer. I know what has to be done about him.

I still need some time to rewrite Vlad's story. I need time to get to the crux of the matter — the inner truth of that strange voice speaking to me through the faded ink.

I have slept for twenty-four hours. I had the strangest dream.

We were standing on the deck of the *Demeter*, Vlad and I. He was facing me and I silently admired his medieval splendor. The pearls on his headgear glimmered brightly. We were both silent. Then he reached out for me, grabbing me by my shoulder. I noticed his fingers for the first time. White, bony fingers with long sharpened fingernails. And his palms — they were as hairy as the backs of his hands.

The grip on my shoulder tightened, and for a

moment I became dizzy and nauseated. I shut my eyes tightly for a couple of minutes before I dared look at him again. For a split second I was staring into his deep-set eyes, and then white fog made everything a blur. Then a sea of flames appeared right in front of me. He had taken me somewhere.

A large building was burning with a thundering, crackling sound. Many voices were crying out in pain and fear like trapped animals. It was terrible but I could do nothing but press my hands against my ears and turn away from the inferno. As I turned around I noticed a figure standing a few feet away. Now I realized that I was actually present at this strange place, not just having a vivid nightmare. I glanced around in wonder and found myself standing on a small hill close to the great bonfire that seemed to feed on human voices. I looked back at the man. It was Vlad, but he didn't see me. Still, I felt his presence and his intentions in bringing me here. I was watching Vlad from a different time and age while Vlad from the *Demeter* was hovering invisibly somewhere around me.

Now I dared take a good look at the man standing there. He was dressed in the same manner as I had seen him on the *Demeter* but his clothes no longer looked aged and worn. They looked brand new. His red coat with the large gold buttons was shining in the light of the flames. The fabric seemed almost alive with different shades of red. I noticed that he was breathing heavily, as if he felt the pain of the burning victims and enjoyed it. The heavy fur collar was wrapped around his shoulders and looked like a live animal. The black pearls and the big topaz on the tight-fitting headgear seemed to reflect the scene of horror going on in front of us.

He didn't even turn his face toward me. How enigmatic he looked with his aquiline nose and closely shaven, protruding chin. His voice sounded inside my head and I recall every word he said.

"Do you know where you are and what you see, Lucia? This is my old fortress burning. The fire is invoking a new era. My regime will not be flawed by the weaknesses and misjudgments of the past. My castle is only a few miles from this place. It took hundreds of aristocrats several years to build it, but now that the work is done it gives me great pleasure to know that the consumers of luxury and splendor actually gave their lives to this magnificent piece of architecture. The few survivors have been released and exiled.

"You are witnessing the last assignment I gave myself before I leave my father's old fortress. I am master in this country. Do you hear the voices, Lucia? They belong to the murderers and thieving vagabonds of Wallachia. They are burning up in the inferno that I prepared for them. Criminals that have done nothing but make life miserable for every law-abiding citizen of this country. They were constantly threatening honest peasants' property and livestock. How can I tolerate that? Well, they will soon be reduced to ashes and bones.

"I have eliminated the major cause of instability and insecurity for people. I have announced the fact that crime of any kind will not be tolerated within Wallachia's borders.

"Follow me and I will show you ..."

I was getting dizzy again. Vlad still had a tight grip on me. I looked around and found myself standing in the middle of a huge square with a large well in the middle and half-timbered, two-story houses all the way around. A man with a heavily loaded wagon was letting his horse drink by the well. A merchant, I supposed.

A group of horsemen approached. Vlad was riding in front, and at the same time I felt his presence inside my head, talking to me in that strange and yet familiar voice. "Pay close attention, Lucia!" he said. "I am showing you my ancient world, and remember that I am still the same though centuries have gone by since this incident. Watch!"

I turned my complete attention to the party on the square. Vlad dismounted and stepped up to the merchant by the wagon. The merchant politely asked Vlad to see that his wagon was guarded during the night. He made it clear that it was Dracula's duty to protect foreign merchants from robbery.

At first Vlad didn't answer the man. He slowly paced around the loaded wagon as if pondering the value of the contents. Then, equally polite, he told the merchant to leave the wagon and assured him that no guard was needed. Instead he invited the man to stay in his castle overnight. The merchant accepted the hospitable offer and went along with Dracula. They disappeared around a corner and I was left alone on the square. It became dark and silent around me.

At dawn (it felt like I had only waited for a few minutes) I saw the merchant appear, followed by Dracula and his guards. The foreigner went straight to his wagon and found that 160 gold ducats were missing. Dracula ordered his guards to replace the missing ducats, search for the thief and announce that the entire city would be burned to the ground if he was not found. Consequently he was produced at once. It was a simple-minded boy who immediately was taken away for execution. Dracula apologized for the inconvenience and, having assured the merchant that his money was replaced, asked him to count it. The merchant started counting, and he counted a second time. Then he turned to Dracula and told him that there seemed to be one extra ducat in the purse.

The twitching of Vlad's lower lip was almost a spasm as he congratulated the merchant and praised his honesty. I noticed the shaking hands of the merchant as he gave the gold coin to Dracula. As the sun glinted on the coin I also noticed the engraving — the Wallachian eagle on one side and the comet with the six burning tails on the other.

I closed my eyes as I was lifted up and taken back to the deck of the *Demeter*. Vlad's hand was still holding my shoulder.

"You see, I would have taken him to the stakes had he not admitted that an extra coin was in the purse. Poetic justice! My servants had spent the night sharpening and oiling a wooden stake in case the merchant proved to be a thief as well. The merchant went on his way, but I am sure that he told the story to everyone who would listen.

"I have always made sure to pay back every injustice. An eye for an eye ... a practice I learned during my stay at Murad's palace. Do you understand me, Lucia? Are you willing to follow me on these conditions? Can you possibly understand the ways of my world?"

Vlad,

You should know by now that I fully understand and accept what you demand. I want to share the privilege of immortality and I long to follow you into the secret darkness of another world. But please note that you are not entirely in charge. Your existence depends on me and my acceptance of what you are trying to communicate through the old papers. Without my pen and my will to take over Maresciu's place in the foggy universe of the *Demeter*, you are nothing. You never give without taking something in return. The same goes for me. We are both approaching a point of transition, just like the beautiful and sad meeting between the maiden and the monster in old horror movies. We will meet at the intersection between your world and mine if we both make an effort to make it happen. We will have to clear the path and dispose of every possible hindrance. You have taken Maresciu out and invited me in. Now I must do likewise.

Arthur arrived last night. I had prepared a nice dinner for him — roast chicken with cheese and a salad. I also found a bottle of Tokay. I am afraid that it completely knocked my friend out. He has been sleeping for almost twenty-eight hours now. But it is not just the wine ...

Delifrena looks like she is quite comfortable sitting on his shoulder. She crawled up there as soon as he had gone to sleep. She has not moved an inch since last night. It is almost as if she is completely stuck to his neck.

I have been up all night. The sun is shining brightly outside but I've made sure the curtain covers every inch of the window. It is actually possible to pretend it is night time in here.

I didn't share the meal with Arthur last night. He arrived late and I told him that I had already eaten. He had the bottle to himself as well. I do not drink myself — wine, that is — and Arthur is well aware of that. I dislike the deadening effect of wine and even food. I feel like I can almost live on my dreams alone. They are becoming more vivid each day.

The little opalescent lamp-globe faintly lit up Arthur's face as he fell asleep, and in the twilight I saw Delifrena sitting close to the white skin of his neck as a little black spot. But sometime during the night she revealed her true nature to me. Her bright green eyes became luminous and intense. For a moment I thought I saw her wink at me, as if we shared some dark secret. She moved closer to Arthur's neck and sat for a long time rubbing two of her front legs against each other. As I watched the two silent figures in the armchair by the window, a soft white fog appeared out of nowhere and covered us in a silky haze. Delifrena's green eyes were shining at me through the haze as I fell back into a world of confused, kaleidoscopic scenes of wonder.

Vlad, you are always entering my rooms when I am awake and waiting for something to happen. But tonight you seemed evasive and incoherent. I couldn't get hold of anything in the dream you brought me. It didn't make sense. I saw that you are capable of extreme actions. A rare sense of justice mixed with gruesome brutality. Maybe you did what had to be done in that old, violent world of yours.

I saw Mehmed's diplomats having their turbans nailed to their heads because they refused to stand before you bareheaded. I heard you say that by this action you hoped to have granted them a favor as they wouldn't have to take off their turbans at all. I also saw you impale a little monk and his donkey as punishment for the monk's claim that you could be none other but the servant of the devil. And there was the peasant's wife who had neglected to repair her husband's trousers. She was impaled next to the monk. But of course you saw to it that the peasant immediately got another wife. She had a good look at the former wife, wriggling on the stake. Then you assured the peasant that this woman would never neglect anything in his household. Not after having seen what could happen to sloppy housewives.

I understand how your mind works. There is a certain pattern. You measure out every punishment according to the crime. You take and replace. But you also showed me scenes of strange beauty. Twilight tableaux on foggy graveyards. Radiant, transparent figures hovering above ground, untouched by the rats squirming beneath. They don't care about the world outside the cemetery. The walls secure their peace. The white marble doves and crying angels of stone sing a perpetual litany accompanied by the whispering sounds from the dancing ghosts.

You have made me understand that life prevails beyond the grave. You have made me very happy.

For a long time I lingered in the dream you sent me. It was perfectly peaceful. When I finally came to my senses it was only a quarter past three. I raised my head and opened my eyes. Delifrena was still sitting on Arthur's shoulder, but her tiny body had swelled grotesquely. Large and throbbing with a red glow coming from within. I tried to move but couldn't. I felt your iron grip pressing me back in my chair. For the first time I felt your presence in my living room. It was terrifying to watch Arthur and Delifrena but I couldn't help feeling absolutely ecstatic knowing that you were in the room with us. It was like those nightmares that freeze your blood in horror but also make you wish that it will never end. The red glow tainted the room, and Arthur's face was a white mask without features in the dark.

Then I felt a rush of cold wind around me. I was lifted up and left floating in midair. My heart was beating violently as Delifrena jumped at me and started to feed me blood. It was revolting, but after a while I started to feel invigorated by the flow of this hot, thick substance. Finally I was let down on the floor again. Delifrena fell down beside me. She looked quite shrunk now. I felt the tension leave the room and noticed the first grayness of dawn slipping through a narrow opening of the curtains. I stumbled to my feet and drew them tightly shut before turning to Arthur. He was still lying motionless, and Delifrena was on her way up to her position by his neck.

I went and got my mercury manometer. According to my reading, Arthur was in a deep coma due to his extremely low blood pressure. In fact, he ought to be dead as a doornail by now but something kept him lingering in this condition of unconsciousness. How strange that I, on the contrary, feel that I never have to sleep again. I am practically glowing and find it difficult to keep still for a second.

What shall I do about Arthur? Or rather, how do I dispose of this deadweight?

July 1, 1994

Arthur is still with me. His condition is the same. He looks like a wax dummy without paint.

I am not sure what will happen next. I know that Vlad is coming again tonight. I can't risk doing anything that will disturb the delicate balance of contact. I don't even dare leave this room because it might break the spell. And besides, I can't walk out the door and face the everyday world. If I leave my dream now, it might be lost for good.

So I stay where I am. Waiting.

WORDS FOR LUCIA

You seem to be familiar with death. You have even studied the decay of flesh, though you turn away from it in disgust. I can understand that, and I approve of you reaching for my world out of fear that you might end up like your parents and their parents. You have learned that my world will never come to an end.

I have been waiting for you a long time. For centuries I have been looking for a kindred spirit. You acknowledge my existence. You seem to know my nature. I have noticed that you have the ability to look beyond what seems to be real and grasp the possibility of the impossible. That is the hardest thing of all. I am familiar with the human way of thinking and feeling but I am only an onlooker. I am not human, and I long to share my secrets with someone of my own kind.

I have lived, and I am not dead.

You have seen my life, and now I want to show you my eternity.

Maresciu's inadequate words told you about the guardian angel of my youth. Castriota. This man expanded my vision and gave me something to believe in. He virtually liberated me from prison and gave me back a life that had been suspended by Murad's devilish plans. And he did even more than that. Castriota was present when I passed from my human life to my eternal existence.

I spent twenty years recreating a civilized Wallachia. I was prince in a country shaken by perpetual divisions and medieval ignorance. However, I didn't make any attempts to enlighten the people of my country. It wasn't wise to shed confusing light on the darkness that they had learned to exist in. Their fear and ignorance made it easy for me to rule. I announced my own laws according to my own rules. My people learned to fear me almost as much as they feared God.

For twenty years I fought the Ottoman Empire. Sultan Mehmed II was an untiring adversary. He constantly craved fame and more Christian land. My brother, Radu, Mehmed's lover and most trusted advisor, had become my enemy. He hadn't left the Ottoman court since he was a child. He never became familiar with his national inheritance and he never claimed it. Radu was caught in the grip of the Ottoman world for life.

Since the beginning of 1476, Mehmed had been working his way as far as Tirgoviste. His army was slowly but surely penetrating my country and he was about to attack my capital city. In the late spring he was close enough for me to see the colors of his standard as I stood on the parapet of my castle. It had cost me dearly to slow him down up to this point and it would be impossible to hold him back now. The time had come for our final combat.

I had made preparations. A mile or so from my castle I had raised a forest of stakes. I knew the sight of them would terrify even the bravest of men. Hundreds of sharpened poles, each carrying its weight of putrefying flesh. During each of Mehmed's little victories, my spies had managed to capture some of the soldiers from the rear party of the vast Ottoman army. For months I had been filling my prison with Mehmed's unfortunate men. When the time came to act, I had them all impaled and left hanging on the stakes. As Mehmed proceeded toward my castle he had the pleasure of the putrid stench for days until he came close enough to see that his own soldiers were the source of it. He couldn't miss the point. The Ottoman garments flapping from the rotting corpses were my special greeting. And as I expected, he stopped dead at the sight. But not for long. He marched on with nothing but my destruction on his mind. Mehmed's army outnumbered my guards and servants, so escape was not an option — an outcome that I had never seriously considered anyway. In fact, I had Mehmed right where I wanted him. Outside my fortress, waiting for the final face-to-face combat.

I started to make plans. The fight was going to be fought on my terms. Mehmed was crazy and impatient, and I knew that if I kept my wits and planned my moves carefully, victory would be mine.

There was a secret passage leading from my private quarters to the ground below the castle and farther on a mile or so into a small wood. This passage would take me behind Mehmed's camp. I disguised myself as an Ottoman scout, intending to play the part of a loyal servant who had just caught up with the army. As you know, Lucia, I spoke the language fluently and I also had thorough knowledge of the Ottoman way of dressing and behaving in front of their leaders. I was certain that the deceit wouldn't present any difficulties.

The plan was to make Mehmed follow me back to the wood and into the tunnel below ground. My soldiers would be waiting in the cellar under the castle where I wanted to face Mehmed in a final duel. I instructed them to guard the entrance and kill his bodyguards should they be with us.

The sun was setting when I made it out of the dark and narrow tunnel. I could see my towers standing as black silhouettes against the red sun. I was sweating, and my heart was beating frantically. I felt sure that I would soon have the satisfaction of running my sword through the sultan's body.

I took a deep breath and gradually became calm. Now I had to take on the part of the brave and loyal scout.

A few minutes later Mehmed's guards saw me approach the camp. I called out an Ottoman greeting and added a secret religious blessing. That satisfied them, and they put down their arrows. As I faced them in the light of the torches they took a good long look at me. I remembered the slightest details of the Ottoman manner of speech, gestures and facial expressions as I started to complain about fatigue and wounds in order to win their trust and draw their attention away from my incomplete attire. Thus I was allowed to walk freely among the Ottoman elite soldiers. Once inside I walked up to Mehmed's tent and told his personal servant to announce me. I made it clear that I had something important to report and that I wanted to see the sultan alone.

This request was granted after some minutes. I went inside and found that my brother, Radu, was present, too. Fortunately, he had retired to the back of the royal tent so that Mehmed could have a private conversation with his spy. I stepped forth and put out my bait.

Mehmed hadn't seen me for years, and he didn't recognize me. I felt absolutely secure in my role as an Ottoman soldier. When I revealed my knowledge of a secret entrance to the castle, he gave me his full attention. I told him that the passage was unattended, as Dracula felt sure that no one knew about it. I also assured him that I had thoroughly investigated the conditions of the tunnel, its length and direction. I hinted that it was possible that the passage was to be used as an escape before long.

Mehmed reacted as expected. He would take any risk to prevent an escape, and he immediately declared that he was ready to follow me to the wood.

Now, I knew that the chances of getting

Mehmed away from his soldiers were extremely small, but since the narrowness of the tunnel only allowed us to walk single file, I hoped to make him go ahead of me. That way I would cut him off from any protection from his guards. Radu was my only concern.

As expected, a large number of soldiers were called — the best of his personal bodyguards and Radu. I succeeded in keeping my face out of the light from the oil lamps, and as we stepped outside and got ready to march, I felt sure that Radu hadn't recognized me. Mehmed was so blinded by hatred that he had gotten quite careless. He never considered the risks of this expedition into enemy ground. He trusted me and felt protected by the mere presence of Radu, his guardian angel. Even Radu seemed blinded by this opportunity to get inside the castle and take the besieged enemy by surprise.

I led them to the tunnel, and as they stood glancing down the dark entrance I made my decision. I was going to take them all down the passage into the darkness, where only I would feel safe and in control.

I turned to Mehmed and asked him if he wanted to pursue this expedition any further. He looked at me with an expression of mad vindictiveness and assured me that he wasn't going to let this opportunity to take Dracula by surprise slip away. Of course, his bodyguards protested strongly but I easily managed to persuade the sultan to disregard the warnings and follow me straight into the castle. So down we went.

As I cautiously pushed Mehmed in front of me, so that I had him completely isolated from the rest, Radu came between us. He stopped his sultan while demanding that I should go first and let him go next so that he could protect Mehmed in case of any danger. My own brother was going to put himself between us as a living bulwark. I couldn't argue with him, and we did as Radu suggested. It didn't matter. It only meant that I would have to kill them both once we were inside the dungeon below the castle. My men had been thoroughly instructed. They would slam the door behind Mehmed and keep his guards from coming to his rescue.

It was a long walk in the damp and cold darkness, but all the way I had the vision of my own face flickering in front of me like a transparent reflection. It was leading me on to the final combat. It occurred to me that something unusual would be waiting for me at the end of the tunnel. An encounter with the dark, liberating forces from another realm. I was going to be united with the secrets that had only been partly revealed to me when I, as a child, had sought another world from the bottom of a pit.

When we finally reached the end of the passage I felt my brother's breath close to me and his drawn sword even closer. He hissed my name and warned me in our native tongue. He had recognized me from the start and had only kept silent because he wanted me to lead them into the castle. He, too, wanted this encounter and now, certain that he was in charge, he ordered me to open the hatchway into the dungeons where his soldiers would be able to act on his orders. They were already starting to push forward from behind, longing to get out of the narrow passage. Of course Radu expected to meet several of my men waiting on the other side of the door, but he felt sure that he would be able to stop them as long as he held me in a tight grip with his sword pressed against my back. I already felt the blood trickling down from the superficial wound he had inflicted on me.

He repeated his order and I opened the door. We stepped inside and Mehmed followed closely while calling his soldiers to attack. We stumbled forward and in seconds my men managed to pull Mehmed in while pushing the Ottoman soldiers back into the darkness. The door was secured and they turned to me for further orders. In the meantime Radu had tightened his grip on me and raised his blade against my throat.

Everyone stopped at the sight. I told my men to stay back as I didn't want them to kill either of my two adversaries. I wanted to fight each on my own terms. It would only be a matter of minutes before the army outside would storm the castle. Under normal conditions my men would be able to hold them back for hours, but this time the Turks had brought their cannons. If, or when, they started to fire against us, the gates would crash almost immediately. Time was running out, but in my mind time didn't exist any longer. I was facing Mehmed while feeling my brother's blade pressed against my throat. I could almost taste their blood.

My men had lowered their weapons and stood silently waiting for me to act. I felt Radu's confusion, and I asked him to fight me in a duel. I then had my men swear that they would release him and the sultan should the outcome of the duel be my destruction. I was lying, but it worked. Radu stepped back and let me draw my own sword. For a moment he staggered back at the sight of Dracul's heavy Toledo blade. His eyes were fixed on our father's sword a second too long, which gave me the opportunity to turn around and plunge the sword directly into the heart of the unsuspecting Mehmed. He fell without a sound and I turned to face my brother. As I looked into Radu's distorted features and hateful eyes, once again it seemed to me that I was facing my own reflection — a hostile image of myself about to lunge forward in an attempt to kill and destroy.

I heard the swishing sound of Radu's sword a split second before it was buried deep in my shoulder. I could feel the blood spurting from the gash and in a flash of pain I lifted my own sword. It seemed weightless, as if the sword was moving by itself. I only had to keep my grip on it and follow its movement. It cut deep into the side of Radu's body, covering the walls with blood. His roar almost drowned out the sound of the cannons, the tumbling walls and splintering doors.

I knew that the Ottoman soldiers would be entering the castle in a couple of minutes, but before they reached the dungeons this battle would be over. My double, or should I say my adversary, was still facing me. I slowly lifted my sword to strike again and watched him do the same. It was like dancing the dance of death in front of a mirror. Both swords went soaring through the air until they met flesh. I felt the cold steel cut through me the second I severed his head.

I was floating without my body. I still had all my mental faculties but I was nothing but my severed head falling to the ground. Radu's own features had returned to his face. My adversary was likewise beheaded, but his eyes were glazed and lifeless.

Dim shadows hovered above me. I knew that they belonged to another world and that they had come to greet me. For a while they waited, staying dim and silent. Then they floated toward me and touched me gently, as if they wanted to let me know that I was going to a place where I could heal and regain my strength.

Meanwhile, my men reacted quickly. I saw my body lying in a pool of blood and watched my loyal servants pick it up. They opened the door of the passage and made sure that it was empty. Mehmed's soldiers had obviously hurried back in order to participate in the storming of the castle. I was lifted and carried along with my body through the long dark passage to the nearby wood. I knew that I was being taken to a place of peace from where I could rise again.

Do you realize what I am saying, Lucia? Death is not real. There is only a temporary condition of help-lessness before entering eternity. Now hear me out.

As I said, I knew where they were taking me. I sent silent messages to my men and I felt that they received and respected my last will. I wanted to be buried next to my father, at the Chapel of Snagov. We reached the end of the tunnel and some of my men managed to steal the best horses from the unguarded camp. My head and body were carefully secured on one of the animals. It would only be one night's ride south to reach Lake Snagov, and I already pictured my friend, Castriota, waiting for me by the chapel on the small island. Finally I had come to an understanding of his never-faltering friendship. From the moment he met me he must have known my destiny and the nature of my being. He and I were bound by a mutual contract, and he was about to perform a last service for me.

The journey went well. We traveled alongside the river Dimbovita and reached Lake Snagov before daybreak. Castriota was there to greet us. I no longer needed to exert myself in order to guide my men's actions. My friend took charge. He immediately ordered them to carry me into the chapel where a bed of wild roses had been prepared by the altar. Candles were lit everywhere and I sensed inaudible voices celebrating a mass for my future existence. Meanwhile Castriota had had the floor tiles behind the altar taken up and a grave dug for me. However, this was only meant for my body. My head was to be laid under the threshold of the chapel. My body was to remain severed according to the rules of what Castriota termed "The Undead."

He had brought my two capes of the Dragon Order — the green and the black. The material was shiny and glimmering, like the scales of a dragon.

The green cape was put over my body. Every silken thread in it felt like living tissue clinging to my skin like a cocoon. The black cape was draped around my head. It was made of a very fine and moist material and I felt part of Castriota's spirit in it. He had made this cape especially for this occasion, and now the energy of a new beginning started to radiate from the black cloth.

As I was laid down they started to cover me with consecrated soil from my father's grave. Heavy tiles were placed above me to cover my resting place, and the last sound I heard was Castriota's voice saying the final prayer.

"The tenth scholar has returned to be united with the forces of darkness. Vlad Dracula's first life has ended, and now he must enter eternity. Let his strength be doubled a hundred times and accept him so that he can participate in the feast of blood."

Then silence prevailed. Even the ground around me was devoid of any sounds. I fell asleep. A sleep without dreams.

LUCIA'S DIARY

July 2, 1994

Vlad,
You fell asleep in your grave below the heavy tiles

of the chapel. Then you rose again, healed and reborn as an immortal being. I watched you kneel by the altar in the dark and empty chapel. The black cape was glowing with a dull, fluorescent light that gave me a hazy view of your profile. It was odd. The cape seemed to light up your face and attract or swallow up the tiny rays of the full moon shining in the windows. A sudden rush of an icy wind swept by me as you wrapped yourself in the black cape and whirled away into the realm of your thousands of lives.

Now I only wait for you to come and take me with you.

It will soon be over. Arthur will wake up again, and when he does he will be alone. When I leave he will be set free. Right now he is caught in the pressure between two worlds still moving closer to each other. We have to get closer. We will meet and perform one last ceremony so that I can detach myself from this life. I know that I must leave behind everything I have ever loved. But I have known that from the beginning of this journey. I will do whatever is needed. I want to renounce the concept of death and live in the dusk where there are no colors except the dim glow of red. Take me back to the deck of the *Demeter*. I am ready. I can already see the old schooner rushing toward me at full sail. I even see your features embedded in the torn canvas.

Delifrena has taken her usual seat on my shoulder. Her little hairy legs are tickling the side of my neck and I am beginning to feel drowsy.

Yes, you can come and get me now. I am ready!

WORDS FOR LUCIA

I got my body back again. Just as you will. An exact imitation of my frail, human body. But this new body is strong enough to resist any of nature's cruel whims. It has no limitations. As long as we drink the blood of others we will remain young and strong enough to challenge time.

In 1894 I made the captain of the *Demeter* take me to England. A hundred years before you learned about me I reached out for you through the mariner Maresciu. You see, I had to make use of a middleman. Through him I reached your kin who faithfully kept the written tale and passed it on to you. My tale seemed baffling and strange to your relatives — I made sure of that! The tale remained a mystery until the moment you read it. You finished it by adding your understanding and acceptance of the truth hidden behind every word.

I spent a hundred years preparing for this encounter. You are impatient, but your waiting is nothing compared to mine. What is a little waiting compared to the incomprehensible eternity beyond your world?

I find you beautiful now, but you will attain even greater beauty when your skin has taken on the special whiteness of the grave. Your pale figure will shine through the darkness when I take you away from the light. You have not yet seen the vast space of my realm nor experienced an existence without any compromises. Go to sleep now. The *Demeter* is lying right outside the field of your vision with her broken masts and torn sails.

LUCIA'S DIARY

I have almost finished my tale. I long for the end. When I write the last sentence tonight I will let go of the world and the life that I know. I leave the old Lucia behind, along with the papers on which she wrote this.

I have slept for the last time. As I was sleeping, a voice ordered me to open my eyes and turn to Arthur. He was opening his eyes, too, only they weren't his pale blue eyes. They were the sparkling green eyes of Vlad looking straight into mine. Now the face changed its features, and the short blond hair started to grow long and turn darker by the second.

After a minute or two it was Vlad sitting in my

living room. In spite of the profound darkness I saw everything as if in bright daylight. He rose from the couch and spread out his arms. I went to him and felt the fabric of the black cape taking possession of my body. It was like being wound up inside a cocoon. My entire being felt like it was being broken apart into little pieces and put together again in a different way. Painful but strangely invigorating.

We whirled away in black softness until I felt the sensation of the slimy deck of the *Demeter* under my feet. My old jeans and cheap shirt had vanished. I was completely naked but I never felt the cold. My vision and my hearing had become sharpened to a degree I would never have thought possible. I noticed every little grain in the rotten, water-stained wood of the ship, and I heard the slow creaking rhythm of the ship's hull. Wonderful music — wedding music!

And the smell. The rotting vessel released its vaporous odors in yellow gushes and I gladly inhaled every breath. It couldn't hurt me any longer. I was safe from death and decay, so why should it bother me?

Vlad was at my side. I felt secure and dominated by his will. I couldn't move an inch as long as he held me in his mental grip. He had thrown away his black cape. He was standing by my side dressed as the ancient prince I had seen in my dreams. He ordered me to straighten up and feel the strength of my new body. I hesitated for a moment. This was a moment of truth. Was it all just a dream?

I took a step forward, and then another. It was amazing to experience a sense of weightlessness in every movement. I felt like a dancer floating in midair. I turned around and faced Vlad. He reached out and took hold of my shoulders. I waited for him to speak but he never said a word. Instead he kissed me, and my mouth was immediately filled with blood. My first drink of life. I felt the warm substance trickling down my chin and my naked body as I drank. Gradually I was covered in red, and to my great astonishment the blood dried and turned into a beautiful dress which I am still wearing. The fabric is smooth and soft and I hardly feel it against my skin.

This was my initiation. And now I am about to turn my back on everything I have ever known. I am going to live forever because I dare to cross the threshold of death. I refuse to accept the facts of death, and by this act of submission to a being that hovers above human life, I will partake of his eternal existence.

But I am taking my memories with me. I will forever be among the shadows that protect the resting place of my family. I am the shadow that gently shrouds every gravestone of my departed kin.

I arrived at my apartment in Copenhagen at the beginning of July, 1994. To my great distress I found the place not only empty but also in an alarming state of disorder. I hadn't received any letters from Lucia for a couple of months but, until my arrival, I had not been concerned. She is an independent and sensible girl, and I thought that she was busy preparing for her exams and otherwise occupied by her friends and boyfriend.

On entering my living room, I was shocked by the sight that met my eyes. The second I saw the incredible mess I knew that something unusual and terrible had happened to my niece. I have never seen anything like it. Not only had the furniture been tossed about as if a hurricane had created havoc inside the building, but also the wallpaper and the ceilings looked as if someone or something had torn at them with monstrous claws. Picture frames were either smashed to pieces or hung upside down on the walls, and broken glass covered the floors. Every single lamp had been crushed.

As I opened the curtains to get some light, I noticed that everything was covered in a sticky white substance — almost like a spider's web, only this substance looked a bit like the surface of a cocoon. It was on every single piece of furniture, and the light made the transparent, silky threads glimmer with all the colors of the rainbow. I had the weird notion that the whole place had undergone some sort of grotesque metamorphosis and that underneath the web I would find my niece. However, as the sunlight started to heat up the clammy rooms, the substance melted and disappeared.

As I stood baffled and confused while the mysterious substance slowly vanished, I caught sight of a small, antique chestnut table. It was the only piece of furniture that hadn't been broken or tossed and it was apparently placed in the middle of the room for me to see. On it lay a heavy bundle of papers that seemed to have been placed there as a special greeting to me. Lucia was not present and none of her personal belongings were left in my apartment. There was only destruction and this bundle of old papers. Could she be responsible for all this?

I can not find a reasonable explanation for the state of my home on that terrible day in July 1994. The strange cobweb was never analyzed. It just vanished like dew before the sun, and like my niece it left no trace behind.

And what about the mysterious bundle of papers? Well, they did offer a rather unbelievable story which Lucia obviously intended to leave, but of course no sane human being could even consider the papers as evidence of what happened prior to my arrival in

Copenhagen. I did read every word carefully, hoping that I might find something to get my investigation started. But the strange tale offers nothing but its own crazy, incoherent world of fantasy. I can see that some of it is written in Lucia's handwriting, but it puzzles me to see that parts of the documents are addressed to her, though the crumpled and yellowed papers are clearly much older than she is. The monstrous being that calls himself Dracula seems to have intended the story of his life to be read by an innocent girl. If I accept this as the truth I shall go as insane as the writing itself, and therefore I refuse to do that. It is the cunning work of a madman. The aged-looking papers must be the result of a lunatic with some knowledge of chemistry. It must be a trick.

However, in spite of my reservations I must rely on what I have seen. How can I ignore the fact that my entire apartment was covered in an unnatural-looking substance? I have seen a lot of cobwebs in my time. I am an expert in this field, but I have never seen anything like this. Somehow it fits perfectly with the diary, which tells of nocturnal meetings with a superhuman being using a spider as a medium. Or did Lucia just imagine it? The police investigations didn't uncover anything useful, and I have spent a lot of time researching on my own.

As I went through every corner of my apartment I did find something unusual. A gold coin. Very old with an eagle engraved on one side. On the other side there is a shooting star with six tails. I know that it might just be an item found in some specialty coin shop but I can't help thinking that it may be an important clue. According to the mariner (or whoever wrote the tale), the coin was stamped at the time of Dracula's second reign. Maybe it is genuine. But how did Lucia get it? Did she find it by accident and manage to purchase it from some ignorant salesman? Is it real, or is it just a copy? It doesn't matter, really. This small piece of gold may have pushed her over the edge. The very notion of something connected with the ancient monster may have had a devastating effect on her mind. It may have pushed her completely into a world of unreality from where she might never return.

Another puzzle worries me deeply as well. Lucia wrote disturbingly about her boyfriend Arthur. It turns out that he left Denmark in June 1994 in order to travel around the world for a couple of years. His family confirmed this and assured me that they receive letters from him regularly. The last letter was sent from a farm in Roumania, where he has been living for a month or so. Nothing indicates that he returned to Denmark during the time Lucia accounts for in her diary. I guess that she must have missed him and that she, in her own twisted way, punished him by placing him in her private world of fiction.

She speaks of a passion strong enough to open the doors of eternity. She writes herself into Vlad's nocturnal world and expresses a wish to become one with him. How can I even begin to understand the way her mind works? I can't seem to grasp the underlying meaning of the multitude of voices crying out from the documents left for me to read. Vlad and Lucia united through the writing — written by whom? — on old yellowed papers. It is an impossible match. And yet she felt the bonds linking her to an ancient figure of doom stronger than her relation to her real, living family and friends. I was the last one of her own flesh and blood and she chose to leave me.

And what about Delifrena, my little specimen that Lucia took care of during my absence? It is quite clear to me that Lucia at some point started to regard the spider as a companion and friend. It went as far as Lucia imagining that Delifrena was acting the part of a medium. The world of fiction entered the world of reality through the work of the spider. Or at least Lucia must have thought so. The spider was knitting a web of fantasy in which my niece became entangled, so to speak.

And where is Lucia now? To which strange place did she travel after leaving her home here in Copenhagen?

I am tired of futile speculations and guesses. I am a scientist and not used to handling anything but facts. Fantasy and dangerous dream-games are mysteries I shall never investigate on my own. I can not and will not try to follow my niece into No Man's Land — if that is where she is now. I just hope that she may return some day. I wish her well.

Wilhelm Mørck